"I won't l

Caden stalk
against the mantel, trying to use his size and his
anger to intimidate her.

But he realized his mistake at once. This close
the scent of her perfume wound around him and
he could see the freckles dotting her cheeks. He
wanted to trace his fingers over the pattern they
made, feel her softness against his rough skin.

And there was something more. A sorrow in her
eyes—a loneliness that called to the empty space
inside him and made him feel a little less like the
outsider he knew himself to be.

He gave himself a mental head shake when her
gaze softened and she swayed toward him. What
was it about Lucy Renner that broke through his
defenses like they were made of air?

* * *

CRIMSON, COLORADO:
Finding home—and forever—in the West

Dear Reader,

Christmas books are some of my very favorite to read and write. There's something about the magic of the holiday season that makes it the perfect setting for renewing hope and finding love.

I'm so excited to welcome you back to Crimson, Colorado, and introduce you to Lucy Renner and Caden Sharpe. Caden is as dedicated to both his adoptive father and the animals he rescues on their ranch outside of town as he is to maintaining his solitary existence. But when Lucy Renner blows into his life like a fierce winter storm, everything he thought he knew about his life and what he wanted from it changed in an instant.

Lucy has had her share of hard knocks and doesn't know what to make of the brooding rancher and the animals he cares for so tenderly. But when she discovers the soft heart beneath Caden's tough exterior, she can't help but fall for him. Both Caden and Lucy have a lot to overcome to claim their own Christmas miracle, and I hope you enjoy reading their story as much as I enjoyed writing it.

I love to hear from readers at www.michellemajor.com or on Facebook and Twitter.

Happy holidays and big hugs!

Michelle

Sleigh Bells
in Crimson

Michelle Major

Recycling programs
for this product may
not exist in your area.

ISBN-13: 978-0-373-62391-4

Sleigh Bells in Crimson

Copyright © 2017 by Michelle Major

Printed in U.S.A.

Michelle Major grew up in Ohio but dreamed of living in the mountains. Soon after graduating with a degree in journalism, she pointed her car west and settled in Colorado. Her life and house are filled with one great husband, two beautiful kids, a few furry pets and several well-behaved reptiles. She's grateful to have found her passion writing stories with happy endings. Michelle loves to hear from her readers at michellemajor.com.

To my readers.
I'm honored and grateful that you make a place
for me and the stories I write in your lives.
May your holidays be filled with peace, joy
and so much love! XO

Chapter One

Lucy Renner pulled her compact rental car to a stop in front of the enormous barn on Sharpe Ranch outside Crimson, Colorado.

If Norman Rockwell and John Denver had looked down from the afterlife to create their perfect town, she figured Crimson would fit the bill to a T. She'd made a pit stop at a local bakery, Life Is Sweet, on her way through the picturesque mountain community. She had been greeted like an old friend even though she felt like an outsider in every way that mattered.

The woman who introduced herself as the shop's owner, Katie Crawford, had not only added an extra shot to the espresso Lucy ordered but then insisted she sample a fresh-baked cookie, still warm from the oven, all the while asking about Lucy's visit to Crimson and plans for the holidays.

But as kind as Katie Crawford seemed, Lucy didn't trust people who were too nice. It meant they wanted something. At least, it did in Lucy's world. Definitely in her mother's world, which was why Lucy's scam radar had gone on high alert when her mom called three days earlier "just to chat."

Her mother reached out only when she needed something. Despite Lucy's resolve not to get mixed up in any more of Maureen's romantic schemes, she'd never been good at saying no.

Now she'd been summoned to the quaint Colorado town that looked like it had puked Christmas cheer all over the place. Much like the rest of downtown Crimson, the bakery had been decorated with festive lights, greenery, ornaments and other vestiges of Christmas, all coming together to make Lucy feel even more grinch-like than normal.

She didn't do Christmas, didn't go in for the magic of the season. She'd worked retail long enough to know that Christmas spirit was a ploy to get consumers to part with their hard-earned cash. She'd had plenty of experience as a kid watching her mother *make spirits bright* in order to further her agenda of the moment. Lucy wanted no part of it any longer. Her plan for the holidays was to survive both the visit and her mother so she could retreat to her boring, quiet life back in Tampa.

Unfolding herself from the car into the biting winter air, she pulled her thin jacket tighter around herself. A two-story farmhouse sat beyond the big barn, situated in the center of a copse of trees, the naked branches swaying in the cold breeze. A cozy stream of smoke rose from the redbrick chimney, and Christmas lights twinkled from a front window as the afternoon light began to gently fade while she stood watching.

She couldn't quite force herself to face her mother yet, not when Lucy's life had become collateral damage in the fallout of Maureen's last romantic catastrophe.

Not when she would have to spend the next two weeks playing a role that made her stomach pitch and twist if she couldn't convince her mom that whatever fantasies she had about being some sort of modern-day frontier wife weren't going to hold up for the long term.

A startled cry escaped her throat as something brushed against her leg. An orange tabby cat wound its way between her ankles then trotted over to the barn and disappeared through the slightly open door. A soft whinny broke the quiet a moment later, followed by an excited yip. Lucy followed the noises and slipped into the barn. Her mother was expecting her in time for dinner, but she had a few minutes to spare and couldn't resist exploring.

She'd taken horseback riding lessons briefly as a girl, paid for by her mother's husband number three. The smell of a barn—the heady mix of hay and animal—had quickly become her favorite scent in the world, and it had broken her heart when she'd had to say goodbye to the leased horse she'd considered hers.

That was when she'd been young and not so careful with her heart, but the smell of the barn still made her happy. It was warmer than she expected thanks to two industrial-sized heaters mounted on the far wall.

This barn was even larger than the one at the farm where she'd taken lessons, with stalls lining either side and a packed dirt floor in between. A horse leaned its head over a stall door and snorted in greeting.

"Hello, there," she said, glancing around but not seeing any sign of human life inside the barn. "Aren't you gorgeous?"

The lights were on overhead and to her right was the open door of someone's office. She peeked her head in at the meticulously ordered desk, but other than stacks of papers, there was nothing in the space to indicate who used it.

Was this the office of her mother's fiancé, Garrett Sharpe, the wealthy rancher who owned the property? She assumed someone with as many business dealings as Sharpe employed a ranch manager, so maybe the office belonged to that person.

Whoever ran the barn was clearly quite tidy. Even the horse tack hanging on pegs in one corner was lined up evenly. Lucy could barely remember to put her wet towel on a hook after each shower.

She spotted a basket of apples sitting on a shelf outside the office and grabbed one, then moved across the barn toward the horse. She heard the stamp of a hoof, and the animal bobbed its head as if calling her closer. He'd clearly noticed the apple.

She held it out in an open palm and the horse snuffled, then took it from her hand. She slid her fingers along the underside of his jaw and up to his neck, loving the feel of the bristly hair under her hands. A high-pitched bark had her turning her attention to the next stall and, suddenly, as if she'd just been discovered, a cacophony of noise broke out across the barn.

She heard barks and yips and a low, mournful yeowing sound and quickly realized each of the stalls was occupied. There were four more horses and at least a dozen dogs, mostly in pairs. She went from stall to stall, visiting with the animals, reaching through the slats of plank siding to pet the ones that came forward to greet her.

At the end of the row of stalls were two rooms that had been built along the barn's outer wall, and she held her breath as she carefully opened one door. The walls of the room were lined with wooden hutches, and a myriad of twitchy noses and bright bunny eyes greeted her.

"What kind of ranch is this?" she asked in a hushed whisper, but the bunnies only hopped back and forth in response.

She reached for the other door, curiosity building in her chest. What was next? Llamas? Alpacas?

Cats.

The second room was filled with cats.

Well, not exactly filled, but there were more than she would have expected, and while she was counting, a small black kitten darted out through her legs.

She closed the door and leaned over to pick up the wanderer, but he crawled under a wide wood shelving unit and out of her reach.

Lucy felt like she'd stumbled on something private here, the animal version of a secret garden or some fairy-tale beast's private castle. She was no Beauty, but whatever this place was or whom it belonged to, she had a feeling she wasn't supposed to be here without permission.

Still, she couldn't leave until she saw the kitten safely back to his cat room, so she got down on her hands and knees and peered under the shelf to the corner where the kitten had lodged himself.

"Here, kitty, kitty," she crooned. The little cat's green eyes focused on her for a second. Then he lifted a leg and started grooming his man parts, which seemed to interest him far more than she did.

"Time for that later," she told him and wedged herself farther into the space. "You look too tiny to be away from your mama, little guy."

"He's seven weeks," a deep voice said from behind her. Startled, Lucy both cried out and lifted her head, banging it hard enough on the shelf above her to see stars.

The kitten dashed past as she struggled to wriggle out from where she'd squeezed herself. Head pounding and blinking away tears, she managed to back into the open space of the barn again. Still on her hands and knees, she looked over her shoulder to find the biggest, baddest-looking cowboy she'd ever seen staring down at her with a deep frown.

The wayward kitten was cradled in the crook of his elbow.

She hadn't heard the man enter the barn but could see the play of light and afternoon shadows from the open door at the far end. Heat colored her cheeks as she realized that the whole time he'd been walking the length of the middle row, she'd been giving him a prime view of the faded jeans that covered her backside.

Way to make a first impression, Lucy.

"Hi," she said, scrambling to her feet and holding out a hand. "I'm Lucy Renner. I'm—"

"The gold digger's daughter," he interrupted in a tone that reminded her of gravel crunching under tires. "You look like her, only not yet as ridden hard and put away wet."

Lucy felt her mouth drop open as her protective streak exploded like a powder keg. Yes, she had problems with how her mother cycled through men, but this would-be Marlboro man, handsome as sin and clearly twice as dangerous, was way out of line.

The man nudged her out of the way as he opened the door to the cat room and dropped the kitten to the ground. "You're also trespassing in my barn."

"You're rude," she said through clenched teeth.

"Doesn't make the words less true."

Dusting off the front of her jacket, Lucy threw back her shoulders and glared at the man. "I don't think Mr. Sharpe would appreciate you speaking about his soon-to-be bride that way."

He started to turn away, and she grabbed his arm, refusing to be intimidated by his hulking physical presence. If there was one thing Lucy could do, it was appear more confident than she was. She had fake conviction to spare, and no way was she allowing some ranch hand to bully her or her mother.

"What's your name?" she demanded. "I'm going to make sure this is your last day working for Garrett Sharpe."

The man stared at her fingers, the pink polished nails so out of place on the dull brown canvas of his heavy coat. Then his gaze lifted to hers, those piercing green eyes as hard as granite.

"Caden," he said so quietly she almost didn't hear him. "My name is Caden Sharpe. Garrett is my—" he paused as if the word was stuck on his tongue "—my father," he said after an awkward moment.

"I thought Garrett's son died a few years ago?" Lucy regretted the question when Caden flinched. Maybe her mother had gotten the story wrong or played fast and loose with the facts to elicit sympathy when she was trying to convince Lucy to make the trip to Colorado.

Family is important to Garrett, her mother had said. *He was devastated by his son's death, and I want to show him I value family the way he does.*

"Tyson." Caden's lips barely moved as he said the name. "Tyson was my brother."

Then, as if her touch was physically painful to him, he shrugged it off and stalked away.

Chapter Two

Caden forced himself to walk out of the barn at a measured pace, even though sweat rolled down between his shoulder blades and his hands shook like the leaves of an aspen tree in a strong wind.

He'd been back on the ranch for almost two years and was so used to everyone in town knowing his story that Lucy Renner's question had caught him off guard.

It brought back all the regrets he had about his relationship with Tyson and how he'd failed the very people to whom he owed his life.

Two years of trying to make up for who he was and who he could never be to Garrett. Trying to keep the old man on track when he would have spiraled into depression after losing his flesh and blood.

A month ago, Garrett had returned from a business trip with Maureen Renner on his arm, a flashy peacock of a woman, so different from Garrett's first wife, Julia, and ridiculously out of place on the ranch. Caden had been suspicious from the start, and when they'd announced at Thanksgiving that they planned to be married Christmas Day, he'd had no doubt Maureen was more interested in

Garrett's bank account than his life as a high-country rancher.

He had two weeks to convince Garrett to call off the wedding, and nothing was going to stop him from that goal. Certainly not a petite, chestnut-haired beauty who smelled like expensive perfume and looked like she belonged at one of the swanky lounges in neighboring Aspen, rubbing elbows with the rich and famous. She did not belong in Crimson and definitely not in Caden's world.

His reaction to her had been unexpected and wholly unwelcome. As much as he wanted to blame it on the view she'd inadvertently given him of the most perfectly rounded hips and butt he'd ever seen, there was something more to it than that.

Caden hadn't felt the powerful pull of attraction in years, not since his desire for a woman had driven a wedge between him and Tyson. Nothing was worth what he'd lost because of love. Or, more likely, it had been lust, which was even worse. Caden had sworn he'd never let another woman affect him that way.

But the immediate wanting—yearning—he'd felt when Lucy lifted those big brown eyes to his had been like an explosion going off in his brain. He didn't want it, couldn't handle it, and it only made him more committed to getting Lucy Renner and her mother away from the ranch for good.

His world would undoubtedly be turned upside down by those two women. He had a routine at the ranch—a mostly solitary existence, especially through the winter—that kept him busy. If it weren't for the barn full of critters that made up his animal-rescue project, Caden could have gone for weeks without seeing anyone but Garrett and the other ranch hands.

In the waning light of afternoon, he checked the outlying cattle troughs, then returned to the barn to feed and water the rescue animals. Lucy's scent still lingered in the air, and his body hardened in response. He forced the image of her out of his mind, focused on his routine and the animals he cared for. Next weekend he was opening the barn for a pre-Christmas adoption event, and he was way behind on preparations for it.

Erin MacDonald, the kindergarten teacher who also ran an after-school program for kids in the community, had convinced him to work with the local humane society to introduce more people to the animals he rescued. He hadn't actually planned on running a makeshift animal shelter. Hell, keeping the ranch going was more than a full-time job. But it seemed as though Caden had been collecting strays since he was a boy.

Maybe because he'd been one until Garrett and Tyson had come into his life.

Once he was certain she'd gone to the house, he finished with the animals, taking time to give some attention to each one. He let the dogs out into the big fenced pen connected to the barn to run and play and couldn't help but smile at their antics.

A light dusting of snow covered the hard ground, and a big storm was forecast for early the following week. Winter on a mountain ranch was a constant battle against the elements and nearby predators, and Caden took seriously the protection of every animal under his care.

Stella, the ranch's cattle dog, had taken on a maternal role with a few of the younger pups, and she nipped at ankles and herded the group of rescue dogs as they ran through the cold evening air, oblivious to the dropping temperature.

Once he had all the animals safely back in the barn, he headed for the main house. Tension knotted his neck and shoulders with every step. He would have much preferred to hunker down in the bunkhouse as a way of avoiding another run-in with Lucy, but he'd promised Garrett that he'd make an appearance at this family dinner.

Golden light spilled from the windows as he approached the main house. Maureen had hung thick swaths of pine rope from the porch railings, decorated with glittering red bows that seemed to draw more attention to the faded gray siding and dull paint of the black trim. He'd climbed those front porch steps thousands of times over the years, but since Tyson's death he'd never been able to step foot in the house without regret washing through him.

"It's about time." Garrett's deep voice boomed from the family room as soon as Caden stepped into the house. "Come in here, Caden, and see how Maureen has transformed this place into a winter wonderland."

Caden sucked in a breath as he entered the family room, with its muted-yellow walls and well-worn furniture. He almost had to shade his eyes at the garish display of Christmas lights strung above the windows and shimmering garland covering the mantel.

"It's pink," he said in horror. It looked like a five-year-old girl obsessed with princesses had decorated the space, not a thrice-divorced woman pushing sixty.

His eye caught on the box marked Decorations that he'd brought down from the attic now shoved into one corner. That box held all the decorations he, Garrett and Tyson had used each year. There were ornaments whittled out of tree branches from the woods on the ranch's south border, along with the small nativity set Tyson's mother had painstakingly painted the year before her cancer diagnosis.

Caden had come to live on the ranch only months after Julia Sharpe's death, and although he'd never met her, he'd felt her presence like a warm blanket at night. In the twenty years since Julia's death, little had changed in the house from how she'd arranged it.

Until Maureen Renner descended on Sharpe Ranch.

"Mom loves pink," Lucy offered from where she stood just inside the room. Color was high on her cheeks. If Garrett didn't know better, he would have guessed she was as put off by the whole display as he was.

"It's a vibrant color," Maureen purred, nuzzling Garrett's shoulder and tracing a manicured hand over his heart. "Bright and alive. This place needed some life breathed back into it."

Caden's adoptive father chuckled as he grinned at Caden. "I suppose you and I have gotten set in our ways living the bachelor life out here. We need a little infusion of spark and color, right?"

"Where the hell do you even find pink Christmas decorations?" Caden asked the room in general.

Garrett laughed again and Maureen darted a dismissive glance toward Caden, then beamed at her daughter. "Remember all the years we decorated for Christmas? You loved putting the star on the tree."

Lucy made a noise that sounded suspiciously like a gag, then cleared her throat. "Sure, Mom. But you're missing a tree."

Maureen opened her mouth but Caden spoke first. "Dad and I will cut one down next weekend." No way in hell was he giving that woman a chance to bring in some fake tree covered in more gaudy lights.

"About that, son." Garrett smiled gently. "Maureen hasn't had much luck finding a wedding dress around here, so I'm going to fly her to New York City for a few days to do some prewedding shopping."

"What?" Caden and Lucy spoke at the same time.

"I need to put together my trousseau," Maureen said, planting a smacking kiss on his father's mouth, "and pick out something special for our honeymoon."

"It's your fourth marriage. What the hell could you possibly need?" Caden pinned the overly made-up woman with a look that let her know exactly what he thought of her, not that it was any secret.

"Caden." Garrett's voice was a warning growl. Caden had heard the tone enough growing up. He'd always been a button pusher and for years had more temper than sense. Tyson had been the one to soften his sharp edges. His brother was always good-natured and smiling. Up until the one fateful argument that had severed their bond.

He wondered what Tyson would have thought about Maureen Renner and her tempting daughter. Well, he could guess what Tyson would have thought about Lucy. She was the type of woman to make a man melt into a puddle at her feet with one glance.

It only made Caden dislike her more.

"Lucy will help you," Maureen offered, her typically brilliant smile tight. "The two of you can put up the tree. She loves Christmas. Traditions are so important to our family."

Another muffled snort from Lucy. "Mom, I came out here because you told me you needed help planning the wedding." Lucy's voice was calm and slightly amused, but Caden noticed her hand was clenched so tightly at her side that her knuckles had gone white. "I can't stay here if you're gone. I need to get back to my life."

Maureen's glossy lips turned down at the corners. "I *do* need you, Lucy-Goose. Especially since we'll be in New York." She placed her fingers on Garrett's cheek and gave him another deep kiss. "My teddy bear and I need a getaway."

"You've got a two-week honeymoon cruise planned," Lucy muttered.

"I've always wanted to see the Rockettes' holiday show," Maureen insisted. "Don't ruin this for me, honey."

Caden saw Lucy's chest rise and fall, as if she was struggling to keep from losing it. "I've got a life in Tampa. I can't ignore it until the new year."

Maureen rolled her big green eyes. "Don't be silly. You haven't had a decent job since you got fired six months ago."

"And whose fault was that?" Lucy snapped.

"It was a misunderstanding that got blown way out of proportion." Maureen gave her daughter a quelling look. "I know you don't blame me."

The air crackled with tension between the two women. "I blame myself," Lucy said after a moment. "For so many reasons."

"I can put you to work," Garrett offered, pulling Maureen even closer, if that was possible. "Maureen said you're real good with finances."

Lucy gave a slight nod. "I have an accounting degree."

"I've been looking for someone to put the books to right on the ranch. Nothing's been the same since Tyson…"

His voice trailed off and Caden closed his eyes, unwilling to bear witness to the pain he knew he'd see etched in his father's gaze.

"Oh, my Lucy's a whiz with numbers," Maureen said, throwing her arms around Garrett's neck. "That would be perfect."

"Not for me," Lucy protested, and Caden felt a strange connection to this beautiful, prickly, unreadable woman. In the barn she'd been fiercely protective of her mother, but here it felt like she was as opposed to this whole charade as Caden.

"I'm happy, Lucy-Goose." Maureen stepped away from Garrett and walked toward Lucy. An image of a coyote approaching a defenseless and cornered jackrabbit sprang to Caden's mind.

He could almost feel Lucy shrink back, although she remained ramrod still. He had the strangest urge to step between the two women and shield Lucy from whatever invisible power her mother was aiming in her direction.

"You want me to be happy. Right, sweetie?"

There was a fraught moment when Caden wasn't sure how Lucy would respond. He could feel the emotions swirling through her from where he stood. Then her shoulders slumped and she whispered, "I do."

Maureen wrapped Lucy in a tight hug and murmured something in her ear that Caden couldn't quite make out. Then she bounced back to Garrett's side.

"I have a lasagna in the oven. Shall we have our first family dinner together?"

"Sounds good to me," Garrett said.

"I have a headache after traveling all day," Lucy told the group, all the spunk and sass he'd heard earlier in the barn gone from her voice. "I think I'm going to head up to bed."

"Take care to drink enough water," his father told her, moving forward with Maureen at his side. "It's easy to get dehydrated at this altitude, especially coming from sea level."

"I will," she whispered. "Thank you, Mr. Sharpe."

"Call me Garrett," his father said with another chuckle. "We're family now."

Not yet, Caden thought. There was still time to turn around this sinking ship, and based on the exchange between Lucy and her mother, maybe an unexpected ally had just arrived on his doorstep.

"You'll join us, Caden," his dad said.

He wanted to refuse, but there was so much hope in his father's eyes. He couldn't disappoint the old man again. Not after everything Caden had put him through in the past and his secret determination to run off Maureen Renner.

Guilt stabbed at his chest when he thought of how sad his father would be when his engagement ended. But Caden had to believe it was better to end things now, before Garrett made things legal. He knew what could happen when his father's heart was truly broken, and he couldn't allow that to happen again.

"I just need to wash up," he told Garrett and earned another wide smile.

Maureen led Garrett out of the family room, toward the kitchen. Caden expected Lucy to move toward the stairs, but instead she walked forward and touched the tip of one finger to several of the brightly colored Christmas lights.

"You can help me stop this," he said into the quiet.

Her shoulders stiffened and she gave a slight shake of her head but didn't turn around.

"Come on," he coaxed, moving closer. "You have to see this for the farce it is."

"Your father seems happy."

Caden opened his mouth to argue, then shut it again. He couldn't deny his dad's upbeat spirit since Maureen had come into his life. In fact, Caden couldn't remember the last time he'd heard Garrett laugh and smile the way he did when Maureen was near.

But that didn't matter. It wasn't real. It wasn't right. And he sure as hell didn't believe Garrett and Maureen were meant to be.

"It won't last," he answered instead. "With her track record, you know it's true. You could talk to her."

She turned to him now, her eyes flaring with emotion he didn't understand. "Does my mother seem like the type to be influenced by anyone else's opinion?"

"She's going to hurt him," he said quietly.

"You don't know that," Lucy shot back, but her gaze dropped to the floor.

Caden muttered a curse under his breath. "*You're* going to hurt him," he accused, lifting a finger and jabbing it at her. "A gold digger and her accomplice daughter. And now my father wants to give you access to his finances." He blew out a breath. "Hell, was this the plan all along? Are you two professional grifters or something?"

"Of course not," Lucy answered, but there was no force behind the words. None of the anger he would have expected at his bold accusation, which made him understand how close he'd come to the truth.

"I won't let this happen." He stalked toward her,

crowded her back against the mantel, trying to use his size and his anger to intimidate her.

But he realized his mistake at once. This close, the scent of her perfume wound around him, and he could see the freckles dotting her cheeks. He wanted to trace his fingers over the pattern they made, feel her softness against his rough skin.

And there was something more. A sorrow in her eyes—a loneliness that called to the empty space inside him and made him feel a little less like the outsider he knew himself to be.

He gave himself a mental head shake when her gaze softened and she swayed toward him. What was it about Lucy Renner that broke through his defenses like they were made of air?

She was dangerous to him and, more important, to his father. The thought of how broken Garrett had been after Tyson died brought Caden back to reality like a bullet piercing his skin.

"I'm going to make sure this wedding doesn't take place," he said through clenched teeth. "Even if my father can't see you for what you are, I do."

Lucy's head snapped back like he'd slapped her. "You don't know me," she whispered.

"But I'm going to," he promised. "Every detail until I expose you and your mother. Mark my words, Lucy Renner. You will not survive me."

Before she could respond, he turned and stalked out of the room.

"You have to let him go." Lucy sat on the edge of the bed in the master bedroom of the main house the following day. "Stop it now, Mom, before it goes too far."

Maureen pulled a dress out of the closet and turned to Lucy, holding it in front of her chest. "For our New York trip, Garrett made reservations at Tavern on the Green. I've always wanted to eat there. It's a landmark, you know? One of the Real Housewives even renewed her vows there. What do you think about this? Too fancy or not enough?"

Lucy sighed. The dress was perfect. It was a deep forest green color with a scoop neckline, fitted without being slutty. Maureen would be stunning in it. Lucy should know. She'd helped her mother pick it out back when Maureen was trying to catch husband number three. "Why Garrett Sharpe, Mom? He isn't your type. Fitting into his life is a stretch, even for you." She pointed to the mounted caribou head above the bedroom's stone fireplace. "Are you going to start wearing camo now?"

Maureen grinned. "Do you know they sell pink camo at the sporting goods store in downtown Crimson?"

"That's not the point and you know it."

"I love him, Lucy-Goose."

The words made Lucy's stomach roil. "I told you after last time—"

"It's not the same," her mother insisted as she folded the dress and placed it in the open suitcase on the bed.

"Of course it's not. Garrett has a son who is both overprotective and beyond suspicious. It's a terrible combination for you. When he finds out—"

"Garrett knows I've been married before."

"That's not what I'm talking about."

Maureen slammed the suitcase shut. "You have to make sure it isn't an issue."

"How am I supposed to do that? The man trusts me even less than he trusts you."

"Don't underestimate your charms, sweetie."

Lucy groaned. "This isn't like when I was a kid and I could be cute or invisible, depending on what your man of the hour wanted. It makes it sound like you're trying to pimp me out."

"Of course I'm not." Maureen gave the suitcase's zipper a hard pull, then let out a little cry. "The dress is caught in it. I've ruined it." She turned and dropped to the bed, covering her face with her hands. "Caden Sharpe is going to ruin everything."

"Don't cry," Lucy said when her mother's shoulders began to shake. She'd always hated her mother's tears. As a girl, she'd done everything in her power to keep Maureen's spirit lifted. It was no easy task, especially after a breakup with whatever man Maureen had fallen in love with in any given month.

Lucy had too many memories of her mother in a weeping puddle on the bathroom floor, but even worse were the times when Maureen was quietly despondent. Those periods of depression had terrified Lucy because she never knew what her mother might do to end the pain.

Maureen was emotionally stronger now—at least, Lucy liked to believe she was. But the sound of quiet sobbing still tore across her chest, and she couldn't seem to stop her panicked reaction that if things got bad enough, her mother might try something desperate.

Lucy gently pried the zipper open and smoothed her hand over the delicate fabric of the beautiful dress. "It's fine. Not even a snag."

"You don't believe I love him." Maureen kept her face buried in her hands.

"I believe you," Lucy whispered. She believed her mother had convinced herself she loved Garrett Sharpe. But Lucy had seen Maureen head over heels too often not to have doubts about how this would end.

Maureen lifted her head and swiped her fingers across her cheeks. "I don't care about his money."

"We both know that's not true."

"It's real this time, sweetie. I promise."

"Have you told him everything?"

Maureen blanched. "I can't. Not yet. He might not understand."

Of course he won't, Lucy thought. A year ago her mother had barely avoided a bigamy lawsuit when it was revealed her third divorce had not been finalized on the eve of what was to be her fourth wedding. Unfortunately, her wealthy boyfriend also happened to be the uncle of Lucy's fiancé.

Lucy still blamed herself. She'd been in love with Peter Harmen and had erroneously thought Maureen would finally step into the role of supportive mother, allowing Lucy to have the happiness and security she'd craved for so many years. That didn't happen.

Maureen had met Peter's uncle, a famed fashion designer and owner of the exclusive boutique Lucy managed in Florida. After a whirlwind courtship even by Maureen's standards—a whole eight days—the two had planned to be married, much to the consternation of the rest of the family.

Then the fact that Maureen was still legally married to Bobby Santino, her third husband and a former professional hockey player, had been revealed. Lucy had never liked Bobby, who had ended up being more of a scam artist than her mother in Maureen's darkest moments. He'd returned before the wedding, attempting to extort money from Maureen to grant her the divorce she'd thought was finalized a year earlier when she'd sent her ex the papers to sign.

Her fiancé had ended the engagement, much to his family's delight, but that hadn't been enough. Peter's cousins had wanted to make a public spectacle of Maureen, making an example of her to warn off any other potential women who thought their father might be an easy target.

To save her mom, Lucy had taken the blame, claiming she'd orchestrated the whole scenario by introducing her mother to the fashion designer and encouraging the courtship as a way to take control of the Harmen fashion dynasty. That couldn't have been further from the truth.

The family had been happy to condemn Lucy as well, and Peter had been pressured to break things off with her by his uncle and cousins. She'd been fired from her job and blacklisted in the retail community. Lucy's burgeoning career had been ruined, but she wouldn't have changed her actions even to salvage her relationship with Peter.

Her role had always been protecting her mother. If she could eke out a bit of happiness or contentment during the times when Maureen was settled, so be it. Otherwise, she was constantly on call, ready to catch Maureen after her many inevitable falls.

Lucy had vowed that the fiasco with Peter would be the last time, but here she was, freezing her butt off in the high mountains of Colorado, the glass eyes of a stuffed caribou gazing down on her as she packed the rest of her mother's things.

"Talk to him," she said softly when she had the suitcase zipped up tight. "Garrett seems like a good man and he clearly adores you. Maybe—"

"Not until after the wedding."

"Has Bobby signed the divorce papers?"

Maureen bit her bottom lip. "He will. He promised."

"Mom, he's a snake."

Maureen stood and walked into the bathroom connected to the bedroom. Lucy heard the sound of drawers opening, then water running from a faucet. When her mother reappeared, a fresh coat of lipstick brightened her smile and she was pinching her cheeks to bring the color back into them. "Help me with Caden." Her voice had returned to its normal raspy, girlish tone, somewhere between Marilyn Monroe and Betty Boop.

"Why didn't you mention him to me before I got here?" Lucy asked, even though she knew the answer. "You made it sound like Garrett's only son had died."

"His older son, Tyson, was killed in a rock climbing accident two years ago. Apparently Caden had been estranged from them both before that."

"Why?"

"An argument over a 'no-good woman' is all Garrett would say about it. I think he was ready to sell the ranch before that, but now that Caden's running things, he feels like he has to stay out here."

"Maybe he wants to stay," Lucy offered.

Maureen shook her head. "He's tired and this was the house he shared with his first wife. She died twenty years ago, and nothing has changed in all that time."

She glanced up at the mounted animal head and shuddered. "He needs a break."

"With you?"

"I *love* him."

It was difficult for Lucy to believe her mother could truly love anyone except herself. But there was no sense in arguing about it now.

"Promise me you'll tell Garrett everything *before* the wedding, Mom. You can't get married until Bobby signs the divorce papers."

Her mom made a face. "Bobby's my past, sweetie. Garrett is my future."

"You can't have a future until he knows. If your love is real, it will survive the truth."

Maureen blinked. For a moment, her eyes lost their guarded quality, and Lucy could see so much hope and vulnerability in them. Her breath caught.

"Do you think so?" Maureen whispered.

"There's only one way to find out."

"You're my best thing, Lucy." Maureen stepped forward and wrapped her arms around Lucy's shoulders. "It's the two of us against the world."

Lucy sighed. "The two of us."

Chapter Three

"She's using you." Caden lifted his father's duffel bag into the back of Garrett's hulking silver truck.

"Have a little faith," Garrett said, clapping a big hand on Caden's shoulder.

"I don't want to see you hurt again." Caden shook his head. "After Tyson—"

"I'm better now." Garrett's blue eyes clouded but he kept his gaze firmly on Caden. "You don't have to worry about me anymore, son."

Son.

That word was like a knife slicing across Caden's gut. Garrett and Tyson had rescued him from the foster-care system and given him the family he'd always craved. But he'd been an angry and stupid kid, constantly pushing boundaries and testing his adoptive father's love because he never truly believed he deserved the happiness he found on the ranch.

He slammed the truck's tailgate shut. "I watched Tyson self-destruct because of a woman and have to live with my part in that. I pulled you back from the brink after his death, and I'm not going to lose you to someone like Maureen Renner." He sucked in a breath when emotion clogged his throat. Then he whispered, "I can't lose you, too."

"You're not losing me." Garrett reassured him in the same gentle tone he'd used when comforting Caden after the nightmares he'd woken from for several months after he'd come to live at Sharpe Ranch. Caden hadn't been willing to let his new father nearer than the foot of the bed at that point. So Garrett had sat on the edge of the sagging twin mattress and talked—telling stories about his childhood or his blissful marriage to Tyson's mother—until Caden had been able to fall back asleep.

Garrett's deep voice had been a lifeline in the dark all those years ago. Now Caden had to squint against the bright morning sun, even though a wide-brimmed Stetson shaded his eyes. It was a perfect Colorado day, with the expansive sky already deep blue. Although the temperature still hovered in the high teens, the sun seemed to warm everything, and the cattle were grazing contentedly on grass and hay in the far pasture.

Caden's heart remained frosty. He'd seen firsthand how much damage a scheming woman could do to a gentle man, and Garrett was one of the kindest souls he'd ever known.

"Think of it as gaining a family," Garrett continued as he hit the remote start on the key fob he held. The diesel engine of the truck roared to life, muffling Caden's disbelieving snort.

"I don't need a family," Caden muttered, and although his father didn't argue with him, they both knew it was a lie. As was true of many kids with tumultuous early lives, Caden craved security and stability like a junkie craved his next fix.

"Tell that to your barn full of rescues," was Garrett's only response. The man never tired of teasing Caden over his penchant for attracting stray animals.

"I'm going to look into her past," Caden said, ignoring the flash of anger in his father's eyes.

"I don't give a damn about her past. She makes me happy, Caden. You should try a bit of happiness on for size. You'd be surprised what a comfortable fit it becomes."

"I'm happy," Caden lied again.

Garrett stepped closer until the toes of their boots touched. At six feet, he'd seemed such an imposing figure the first time Caden had visited the ranch. Now Caden was at least three inches taller than him, but Garrett still remained a force to be reckoned with. "You *deserve* to be happy."

Caden tried to hold his father's gaze but turned away after a moment. How could Garrett say that, let alone believe it, when Caden was the reason Tyson was gone?

"Take care of Maureen's girl while we're away."

Caden swung back, grateful to have a reason to let his temper fly. "She doesn't belong on the ranch, and she sure as hell doesn't need access to your finances."

"I met with her this morning. She's got a good head on her shoulders. I've lost track of the business side of things recently. That's the part Tyson handled and—" The old man pursed his lips and ran a hand through his thick crop of silver hair. "Anyway, it's good to have fresh eyes reviewing things."

"More like a fresh attitude." Caden kicked a toe into the dirt. "I don't trust her, either."

"Give her a chance," his father coaxed. "It makes me feel better to know you won't be out here all alone."

"Chad's here," Caden said, referring to the young bull rider who worked winters on the ranch. "He's company."

"Chad's too busy in town chasing women." Garrett wagged a finger. "You could stand to go in with him a time or two. It's amazing what a difference it makes having a woman in your bed at—"

Caden held up both hands. "Stop before you make my ears bleed. I don't want to hear about my dad's romantic escapades."

Garrett chuckled. "You could learn something, young man. Be nice to Lucy. She's important to Maureen which makes her important to me."

Caden's jaw tightened at the thought of spending any more time than necessary with Lucy Renner, but he nodded. He'd learned from a young age there was no point in arguing with Garrett Sharpe when the man had his mind set on something. Caden was just going to have to prove what a mistake marrying Maureen would be. And he had two weeks to do it.

Later that afternoon, Lucy stood looking out the main house's big picture window, taking in the snow-covered peak of the mountain looming in the distance and the expanse of open fields that surrounded the property. She'd lived in Indiana until the age of eleven when Maureen had transplanted them to Florida for husband number two.

Lucy liked the change of seasons, but the thick white snow that blanketed everything for miles was a revelation. It was difficult to believe animals could survive outdoors in this climate, although the serenity of the scenery spoke to something deep in her soul. Colorado felt fresh, clean and full of new promises, which she assumed was part of the allure for her mother.

Maureen loved nothing more than to reinvent herself with each new adventure that came along. Lucy found herself reluctantly smiling at the thought of her mom herding cattle or churning butter or whatever it was ranch wives did these days.

It had been hours since the happy couple had driven off toward the regional airport, where they'd board a private plane to take them into Denver to catch a commercial flight to New York City.

"First-class," her mother had whispered into Lucy's ear as they stood in the driveway earlier, saying their goodbyes. "I haven't flown first-class since Jerry." Maureen's marriage to husband number two, Jerry Murphy, had lasted only a few months, but Maureen had made the most of her time with the wealthy restaurateur from Naples, Florida.

Lucy had seen Caden's shoulders stiffen and guessed that he'd overheard Maureen. Great. One more reason for Caden to mistrust them. How could Lucy explain her mother's childlike immaturity when half the time Lucy didn't understand it herself?

Garrett seemed to take it all in stride, and Lucy got the impression he tried to be purposely over-the-top to illicit a reaction from Maureen. There was something inherently magnanimous about the older rancher, as if he enjoyed having someone with whom to share the trappings of his wealth.

As soon as the truck had disappeared down the long, winding drive that led to the highway, Caden turned and stalked away.

Lucy returned to the main house and wandered from room to room, imagining life here before the force of nature that was her mother descended. How did a father and son, a widower and a bachelor surrounded by the memories of a beloved wife and brother, spend their evenings?

From Garrett's effusive compliments about her mother's cooking, he wasn't accustomed to home-cooked meals. Lucy could relate to that. The only time her mother had ever cooked when Lucy was growing up was when Maureen was trying to impress a new boyfriend.

She moved toward the bookshelves in the family room, which were filled with volumes on outdoor life and classics she'd expect a man like Garrett to read— Hemingway and Twain—with the occasional modern thriller thrown in for good measure. A collection of framed photos took up an entire shelf, and she could piece together the Sharpe family history from the faces smiling out at her.

There was one of a beautiful young woman holding a toddler, who grinned widely and wore cowboy boots a size too big for him. The woman's hair was pulled back into a low ponytail and she wore no makeup, but she didn't need any. She stood in front of a split-rail fence with a dozen cattle grazing behind her.

The next photo showed the same boy, who Lucy assumed was Tyson Sharpe, as a gangly adolescent with his arm slung around Caden's shoulder. Lucy could easily recognize his mutinous scowl, although in the photo he was all gangly arms and skinny shoulders. He was glaring at the camera, a fact that his brother seemed to enjoy immensely.

Another photo showed both Tyson and Caden wearing graduation gowns and caps, Garrett with an arm wrapped around each of them. Caden had started to grow into his body by that point, and Tyson had also become a wildly handsome young man with thick blond hair and a careless grin so different from that of his brother's tight smile.

Lucy's breath caught at the final photo. It showed Tyson and Caden at the base of a sheer cliff, both wearing climbing gear. Caden was a few inches taller than his brother, but what punched at Lucy's chest was the pure joy displayed in the photo.

Caden's head was thrown back in laughter, and Tyson was grinning and looking at Caden with a good bit of love and adoration. The bond between the brothers had clearly been solidified at that point. At least in the second the photo was snapped, Caden had dropped his defenses to revel in whatever moment they were having.

She couldn't help but be curious as to the circumstances of Tyson's death and why Caden seemed to take the blame for it. She wished she'd asked her mother for more details, although there was a good chance Maureen wouldn't be aware of the situation since it didn't affect her directly.

The sound of the front door opening and male voices coming closer interrupted her musings. She whirled away from the bookcase and took two hurried steps toward the middle of the room, feeling somehow like she'd been spying on Caden by looking at the photos.

He appeared in the hall a moment later, and color rushed to Lucy's cheeks as his stark gaze landed on her. She cursed her pathetic and weak body, which reacted to the way he was studying her with an involuntary shiver.

How was she supposed to keep her distance from this man when she could almost feel the current of attraction pulsing between them?

"Are you casing the place now that my dad's away?" he asked drily, offering an acute reminder of why it would be easy to stay away from him.

Because he was a jerk.

"You must be Maureen's daughter," the other man said and strode forward to take Lucy's hand. She guessed he was younger than Caden by at least five years. His light blond hair fell over hazel eyes that were wide and welcoming. "Your mom is awesome. She's pretty hot, too. A real MILF—"

"Chad." Caden's voice was like a slap, cutting off Chad midsentence. Lucy had to admit she was grateful. She should have been used to how men both young and old reacted to her mother. Yet it still made her as uncomfortable now as it had when she was a kid. There were many years she'd lied to her mother about school activities just to avoid Maureen showing up in her plunging necklines and thigh-grazing hems to flirt with unsuspecting teachers or the fathers of Lucy's few friends.

The younger man chuckled. "Sorry," he said, although he didn't look the least bit apologetic. "But, sweetheart, you clearly inherited your looks from your mama."

"I'm not your sweetheart," Lucy said softly, earning another chuckle from the man.

"Not yet, anyway," he said with a wink.

Lucy rolled her eyes but felt the corners of her mouth curve up. There was something so inherently charismatic about Chad, not to mention how handsome he was. In his tight jeans, cowboy boots and fitted flannel shirt, he reminded Lucy of a young Brad Pitt circa *Thelma and Louise.*

Not that she had any intention of driving her car over the edge of a cliff or getting involved with an obvious player like Chad. But it was fun to be on the receiving end of that thousand-watt smile, especially when Caden was looming at the far end of the room, glowering at the two of them.

"I'm Chad Penderson and I work here at Sharpe Ranch."

"I'm Lucy Renner."

"Pleased to make your acquaintance, Miss Lucy." He took a step back and gave her a courtly bow. "If you need anything while you're here, just let me know." He straightened again and wiggled his brows. "I do mean anything."

Lucy heard something that sounded like a growl from Caden, but Chad's grin only widened. "How long are you staying at the ranch?"

She shrugged. "The plan is for me to stay through the wedding. Garrett has asked me to go over the books and—"

"Not necessary," Caden interrupted, stepping forward.

She bristled at his dismissive tone. Lucy had spent too much time being dismissed to ever let it pass without a fight. "That's not what your father seems to think."

"We have a financial manager who's taken over the accounting since…" He paused, then said, "For the past couple of years. He's immensely qualified."

He didn't add the words *unlike you*, but Lucy felt them linger in the air just the same.

"You can hang out with me," Chad offered. "It's quiet

around here in the winter but there's plenty of work to go around. You know how to ride a horse?"

"Not really," Lucy admitted.

"Then I can teach you."

"She's not learning to ride with you," Caden said, his voice pitched low.

"Listen to Mr. Party Pooper back there." Chad hitched a thumb in Caden's direction. "Speaking of parties, I'm meeting some friends in town tonight for a little pre-Christmas bash. Why don't you join us?"

Lucy shook her head. "I don't think—"

"Come on," Chad coaxed. "You'll have more fun with me than stuck out here with Caden." He threw a glance over his shoulder. "No offense, boss, but you're about as much fun as mucking a hog pen."

"She's not going with you. Grab a cup of coffee and let's finish fixing the heater before the water freezes."

"As in, we won't have running water?" Lucy asked, trying not to sound panicked. She was by no means spoiled but definitely enjoyed a hot shower on a cold morning.

Chad winked. "We have to keep the water troughs heated for the cattle."

"Can't they eat snow?"

"No, darlin'. One of the biggest threats to livestock in the winter is the cold. The snow lowers their body temperature, which could be deadly. Our job is to keep them warm and safe."

"Oh."

Caden folded his arms over his big chest. "Your job is not standing in the house jawing all afternoon, Chad. You wanted a cup of coffee. Get it and let's go."

"If you change your mind about tonight, I'll be leaving here around seven." Chad pointed out the window toward a smaller structure about ten feet behind the main barn. "I'm out in the bunkhouse." Another wink. "For your information."

"She's not going," Caden repeated, glaring at Lucy over Chad's shoulder.

If there was one thing Lucy hated, it was being told what to do. By anyone. It had led to some monumentally stupid decisions on her part, but it was a part of herself she couldn't seem to rein in.

"I'd love to go to your Christmas party," she told Chad, offering a slight smile.

"Hot damn," the young cowboy said, slapping his knee. "I've got me a date."

He shot Caden a gloating smile. "You hear that, old man? Miss Lucy here is going to be my date for the evening."

Caden said nothing, but Lucy could almost see the smoke curling from his ears.

"I'll see you later, darlin'," Chad crooned before leaving the room.

Caden didn't move, just continued staring at Lucy.

"Of course it's not a date," she said after a moment, pulling at the hem of the pale pink sweater she wore. Having lived in Florida for so many years, she had very little in the way of warm clothes and wondered if there was any discount shopping to be found in Crimson. "He's far too young for me."

"That won't matter to Chad." Caden spoke through clenched teeth. "Don't let the aw-shucks act fool you. That boy is a player."

Lucy wasn't sure whether to be offended that he hadn't denied she was too old for Chad or flattered that Caden was, in his own awkward way, trying to protect her from being hurt. "I'm not in the market for getting played. You don't need to worry about me."

He looked as though he wanted to argue, but said, "I wasn't kidding about the ranch finances. One of Tyson's friends from high school who's a CPA has taken over since..."

"Since your brother died?" she asked gently.

"Yeah."

"My mom told me it was a rock climbing accident. I'm sorry."

Once again, Caden's silence stretched so long she thought he might not respond. He looked past her, out the window into the darkening night. His green eyes filled with so much sorrow that Lucy felt an answering pull of sadness in her chest.

"I'm the one who's sorry," he said finally. "His accident was my fault."

Lucy gasped, and Caden's gaze shot to hers. All the vulnerability that had been there moments before was gone, his expression carefully blank.

"You don't belong here," he said, his voice so low she had to strain to make out the words. "I'll hurt you whether I want to or not. It's what I do."

Then he turned and walked away.

Chapter Four

Caden pulled open the door of Elevation Brewery later that night, the heat and noise of a festive bar crowd spilling out into the cold. He took a deep breath, then walked in, scanning the faces of the people without making eye contact with any of them.

"Caden!"

He stifled an amused sigh and turned to the dark-haired, dark-eyed woman waving to him like mad from a seat at the bar.

"Caden, over here!" she shouted as if he hadn't heard her the first time.

Out of the corner of his eye, he saw Lucy Renner glance over her shoulder. But he ignored both Lucy and Chad, who were huddled together near the pool tables at the far corner of the bar, and moved toward the woman still feverishly waving at him.

"He sees you," David McCay, the bar's owner, told Erin MacDonald as Caden approached. The tall brewer with the overly long blond hair and a good two weeks of beard leaned forward to plant a kiss on the mouth of his fiancée.

"I didn't think he'd come," Erin said against David's lips before swiveling her chair to face Caden. "I'm so glad you finally took me up on my offer."

Caden blinked, looking around like one of the other bar patrons might be able to shed some light on what the sweet-tempered schoolteacher was talking about. Because he sure as hell had no idea.

David gave a soft chuckle. "He's not here for you, darlin'."

"I texted you about meeting here to talk about the animal-adoption open house next weekend." Erin pointed a finger at him. "You've ignored my invitations to hang out with David and me for weeks. I figured bringing the animals into it might motivate you to agree. That's why you came tonight, right?"

"Um, sure." Caden's gaze strayed to Lucy, who was leaning over the pool table to set up a shot. Several of the men standing near her were watching her with interest, but Chad had his arm draped around the shoulder of a buxom blonde.

He started when Erin placed a hand on his arm. "I'm not going to be offended that you ignored me once again because this is even better. You're here for a woman."

"I'm not," he answered, but Erin was craning her neck to get a better look at Lucy.

"She's pretty. Not from around here, I'd guess. Tell me all about her."

Caden shot a help-me glance toward David, who gave him a you're-on-your-own shrug.

"There's nothing to tell," Caden said with a sigh.

"Come on." Erin grinned up at him. "You never come into town, especially on a Friday night. She must be special."

"She's here with Chad. It's not a big deal."

"I don't think she's leaving with Chad," David said, inclining his head toward the back of the bar.

Caden turned to see Chad and the blonde in the midst of a hot and heavy makeout session. Lucy was on the other side of the pool table, talking to a group of men, some of whom Caden recognized as locals. A moment later Chad and his new woman came up for air, then quickly headed for the bar's entrance. His ranch hand disappeared into the night without sparing another glance at Lucy.

"Damn," he muttered. "I tried to warn her."

"Were they on a date?" Erin asked, sympathy lacing her voice.

"I don't think so. Maybe. Hell, who knows with Chad? But he was definitely her ride home."

"So now you'll take care of her," Erin said matter-of-factly. "And you can tell us all about how you two met."

"It's not important."

Erin let out a sigh. "Fine. If you won't share, maybe she will." She stood on the stool's footrest and waved Lucy over when she glanced up, presumably looking for Chad.

Caden saw confusion darken her eyes, and then something else crept in when her gaze landed on him. But she moved toward them, weaving her way through the brewery's high-spirited patrons.

Several male heads turned as she passed, but she didn't slow her progress.

"She's not my responsibility," he said quietly.

"*She's* the reason you're here," Erin responded. "Gosh, she's even prettier than I first thought."

"Not nearly as pretty as you," David whispered.

"You're sweet," Erin told her fiancé, but Caden barely registered their conversation.

He couldn't take his eyes off Lucy.

Her dark hair fell over her shoulders, and she wore a burgundy-colored sweater with the fabric cut out at both shoulders, giving him the most tantalizing glimpse of bare skin. It was totally inappropriate clothing for a December night in Colorado, and Caden thanked his lucky stars that Lucy came from a warmer climate.

"So you're not a party pooper after all," she said as she came to stand directly in front of him.

He cocked a brow. "I told you a date with Chad was a bad idea."

"I told you it wasn't a date."

"Obviously not since he just left with another woman."

"Oh." Her glossy lips formed the syllable and Caden's body tightened in response.

"He ditched you, Lucy." Caden knew he was being purposely cruel, but he couldn't seem to help himself. It bothered him on some primal level that she'd gone out with Chad, and he certainly planned to have a serious conversation with his ranch hand about how to treat a woman.

"Was it the cute little blond-haired woman?" Lucy asked.

"Yeah."

"Good for him," she said, a slow smile lighting up her face. "Her name is Jessica and he has such a crush on her. All I heard about most of the night was how she's been dating some guy who doesn't treat her right. She finally broke up with him last week. Tonight was

Chad's big chance but he was so nervous. I gave him some tips and—"

"You and Chad were over there talking about how he could put the moves on another woman? The last thing that boy needs is more moves."

"He *really* likes her," she said. "I get that he seems smooth, but it's different when the woman means something, you know?"

Caden wasn't sure how to answer that. He thought he'd been in love once, but that experience had not only torn apart his heart, it had done some major collateral damage to his relationship with his brother.

"I know exactly what you mean," Erin said from behind him. She nudged his shoulder and he stepped to the side so that Erin could pull Lucy closer. "Why do men act like idiots when they have real feelings for a woman?"

"I wasn't an idiot," David protested gently.

Erin rolled her brown eyes toward the ceiling. "You were a total idiot." She reached for Lucy's hand and pumped it enthusiastically. "Hi, I'm Erin MacDonald and this is my fiancé, David McCay." She leaned in closer and added, "He's a reformed idiot."

"Can I get you a beer?" David asked Lucy with a chuckle.

"He also owns Elevation Brewery. We're friends of Caden's."

Lucy gave Caden a funny look out of the corner of her eye, as if she found it difficult to believe he actually had friends. "Nothing more for me," she told David. "I had a couple of pints of the wheat beer earlier—which was amazing, by the way. But I'm definitely feeling the altitude."

"The alcohol hits you hard up here," David confirmed.

"Caden was just about to tell us how the two of you met," Erin said.

Lucy arched a brow in Caden's direction. "Really?"

"It would probably be better coming from you." Erin placed a hand on Lucy's arm like they were old friends. "Our Caden is kind of the strong, silent type, if you know what I mean."

"My mother is marrying his father," Lucy said, thankfully not commenting on what she thought about his "type."

"Maybe," he muttered, earning a frown from both women.

David handed him a tall glass of dark beer. "You look like you could use this."

"I've seen her around town," Erin told Lucy. "She and Garrett seem so happy together. She's really pretty. You look like her."

Lucy's gaze strayed to Caden once again, her eyes narrowing slightly as if she was thinking about the rude comment he'd made when they first met.

Then she smiled at Erin. "Thank you. My mom and Garrett left this morning for a prewedding trip to New York City."

"How romantic," Erin breathed.

Caden snorted, causing beer to slosh over the side of the pint glass. David handed him a napkin.

"Will they be back for the adoption open house?" Erin asked, turning to Caden.

"Doubtful. I'm guessing Maureen will want to stay in the city and spend as much of Garrett's money as she can manage."

Erin gasped. "That's a rude thing to say, Caden. And unlike you. You know better than most people what it's like to be judged unfairly. I'm disappointed you'd stoop to that level, especially talking about Lucy's mom when she's standing right in front of you."

"Sorry," Caden mumbled, feeling suddenly like he was a kid being reprimanded by his favorite teacher. He could only imagine how bad the kindergarteners in Erin's class felt when they messed up. Erin might look like she was as harmless as a kitten, but she definitely had sharp claws.

David covered his mouth with one hand to hide a smile while Lucy raised a brow and moved slightly closer to Erin, as if her new friend would shield her from Caden's wrath. He gave himself a mental head shake as guilt pinged through him. Still, he hadn't said anything about Lucy's mother that wasn't the truth, and they both knew it.

He placed the glass of beer on the bar. "We should head back to the ranch."

Lucy crossed her arms over her chest. "What's the adoption open house?" she asked Erin, ignoring Caden.

"Have you seen Caden's pet-rescue operation?" Erin rolled her eyes. "When he's not being Mr. Rudepants, Caden takes in unwanted animals from around the county."

"The ones in the barn?"

Erin nodded. "They're animals no one else wanted. He rehabilitates them, does training and then matches them with forever families."

He saw Lucy's mouth drop open. "Seriously?"

"Did you think I was selling them to some kind of lab

for experiments?" he asked, not caring that the words came out a growl.

"No," Lucy answered after a moment. "I thought you were a pet hoarder."

"Are you kidding me?"

She flashed a grin that made his heart stutter. "Yes."

She turned back to Erin, who was watching him with a gleam in her eye Caden didn't trust in the least.

He picked up the beer again and took a long drink.

"Erin's onto you," David said quietly as Erin explained more about the open house to Lucy. "You need to get a better poker face, bud."

Caden stepped closer to the bar. "I don't know what you're talking about."

"You like this one."

"She's a pain in my—"

"Right." David laughed. He made a show of wiping the already-gleaming wood counter when Erin shot him a questioning glance. "You should probably stop staring at her like she's on the menu and you're starving."

"I'm not staring."

"Erin has been wanting to fix you up for months. She fancies herself a matchmaker."

Caden groaned. "I'm trying to convince my father to call off the wedding. That's not exactly going to endear me to Lucy."

"Doesn't change the fact that you like her," David said with a shrug.

Before Caden could respond, Erin turned and grabbed his arms.

"Great news," she shouted over the din of the brewpub. "Lucy's agreed to help with the adoption event."

Caden shrugged off her hold and shook his head. "I didn't ask for her help."

Erin frowned. "Don't be rude again."

"I'm not—"

"You need her."

"I don't," he said through clenched teeth.

Erin pointed a finger at him. "How much of the marketing plan I created have you implemented at this point?"

"I've been busy on the ranch."

"Exactly. Lucy has retail experience in sales and marketing. She's going to take over for you to make sure we have enough publicity for the event."

Caden looked over Erin's shoulder to Lucy. "If you don't want my help," she muttered, "it's not a big deal."

"It *is* a big deal," Erin insisted. "Ever since word got out that Caden would take on stray animals, people have been bringing them to him left and right. It's too much. An adoption event right before Christmas is the perfect way to find good families for your sweet babies."

Caden felt color rise up his throat when Lucy's mouth kicked up at one corner. "I wouldn't call them my sweet babies."

Erin threw up her hands. "You have a certified therapy bunny, Caden. Play the hardened cowboy all you want, but we know you're a big softy at heart."

"We do," Lucy agreed, her eyes dancing with amusement.

"I don't even know why I agreed to open the barn. I can find homes for the animals on my own."

"The adoption event is happening, and Lucy's going to help," Erin said in the same tone of voice he imagined she used to quiet a room of rowdy five-year-olds.

Caden looked at David. "You've got your hands full."

"Wouldn't have it any other way," David answered.

"I'm so glad we met tonight," Erin said to Lucy as she pulled her in for a tight hug. "I have a feeling we're going to be great friends."

Caden's focus sharpened as he watched Lucy go stiff. All the humor disappeared from her gaze, and instead she looked like someone had just punched her in the gut.

"It was…um…nice to meet you," she said quickly. "But I'm kind of jet-lagged, so I should probably head back to the ranch. Have a good night."

She turned and fled, weaving through the crowd so quickly that Caden lost sight of her within a few seconds.

"Was it something I said?" Erin asked quietly.

"Nah, honey." David reached across the bar to smooth his fiancée's hair away from her face. "You were brilliant. I'm just not sure Caden's Lucy is used to having someone as sweet as you offer to be her friend."

Caden felt his jaw clench. "She's not mine."

"Not if you don't catch up to her," David agreed.

Caden knew the smart thing to do would be bellying up to the bar and ordering another beer. Lucy Renner seemed plenty capable of taking care of herself. He sure didn't need her infringing on his life, his friends or his animals. He needed her gone.

He took a breath and turned to find Erin and David staring at him with equally knowing looks on their faces.

"Damn," he muttered and took off toward Elevation's front entrance.

It had started snowing while Lucy was in the bar. Big, fluffy flakes streamed down from the sky, glowing in the light of a nearby streetlamp and lending a sense of peace to Crimson's Main Street. Lucy would have stopped and tipped up her face to catch a snowflake on her tongue if she wasn't in such a hurry to get away.

She felt like a fool rushing out of Elevation and away from a woman who'd been nothing but kind to her. When was the last time Lucy'd had a girlfriend?

She almost laughed out loud at the thought. Her mother had always taught her that other girls, and later women, were to be viewed as competition and not to be trusted.

As much as Lucy knew her mother's ideas on female friendships were wrong, some part of the message had sunk in and she'd never seemed to be able to make lasting friendships. Maybe because whenever another woman made a friendly overture, she freaked out like she did with Erin.

At least Caden was probably happy she was gone.

Of course, she had no idea where she was headed. She needed to get her bearings and find a taxi or Uber to get her back to the ranch. But it was hard to slow down when it felt like running away was what she did best.

Heavy footsteps sounded on the sidewalk behind her, and she glanced over her shoulder to see Caden approaching. She hated to admit how happy she'd been to see him at the bar.

Chad and his friends were fun, but they were immature boys compared to Caden. Even though he'd never been anything but gruff and rude with her, she felt an odd sense of comfort when he was around.

As usual, he was scowling when he caught up to her. "Where's your jacket?" he demanded.

She looked down at the thin sweater she'd chosen for the night, along with skinny jeans and ankle-high boots that allowed a tiny strip of skin to show below the hem of her jeans. It was amazing how cold that little bit of exposed skin had gotten already.

Caden, in contrast, wore dark jeans, well-worn cowboy boots and a heavy canvas jacket that looked deliciously warm. She shivered as his gaze raked over her, and she wasn't quite sure whether it was in response to the cold or the intensity of his green eyes.

"I didn't wear one."

"Are you trying to catch your death of cold?"

Lucy clapped a hand over her mouth when a giggle bubbled up unexpectedly. "You sound like a grandma."

"At least little old ladies have the common sense to wear a coat in Colorado in the middle of December."

She shrugged. "We were going to a bar in Chad's heated truck. I didn't think I'd need a coat." At the mention of heat, her body seemed to register the below-freezing temperature of the winter night. A shiver coursed through her and her teeth started to chatter.

"Let's go," Caden ordered, unbuttoning his heavy coat and wrapping it around her shoulders. She almost sighed as the residual warmth from his body enveloped her.

"You don't have to do that," she said even as she pulled the jacket tight around her.

"My dad will kill me if I let you freeze to death." He took her elbow none too gently and began to steer her toward a dark gray truck parked next to the curb.

"I'm fine on my own. I can call a cab."

He laughed. "In Crimson?"

"Or I'll Uber a ride."

"Don't read too much into this. We're going to the same place. I can drive you back to the ranch. I'm not asking you to wear my high school ring."

Caden held open the truck's passenger-side door as she climbed in. He might not like her, but this cowboy was a gentleman. Lucy couldn't remember ever being with a man who had such decent manners.

"Do boys still give their girlfriends a class ring to wear?" She pulled the seat belt around her and giggled again. "Or letter jackets? Is this canvas coat like the ranch version of a high school letterman's jacket?"

Caden leaned closer and stared into her eyes. "Are you drunk?"

She pushed him away. "No. I had a couple of beers when we first got to Elevation."

"Talking nonsense is a symptom of hypothermia." He slammed the door shut before she could respond. A moment later he climbed into the driver's side and turned on the car.

"I'm not hypothermic," she said through her teeth as he cranked up the heat and adjusted the vents to blow on her. "It was a joke."

His hand stilled for a moment, and he glanced over at her as if he was unfamiliar with the concept.

"Chad shouldn't have left you," he said, pulling out into the middle of the deserted street.

"I haven't seen snow like this for years," Lucy told him, ignoring the comment about the young ranch hand. Truly, she was happy Chad had made the connection with the girl he wanted. There was something about the snow that made the night feel particularly intimate, and someone should be taking advantage of it.

"How long have you lived in Florida?"

"Mom and I moved from Indiana when I was eleven."

"Why?"

She hesitated, then admitted, "She'd met someone at the restaurant where she worked. Jerry had come to Indianapolis for business."

"Husband number two or three?" Caden asked quietly.

"Two." Lucy sighed. "He was a good man. He treated me like a real daughter."

"But it didn't last?"

He asked the question casually, but she couldn't help but wonder if he was digging for information to use against her mother. "They wanted different things from life."

Caden arched a brow but didn't say anything else. She pressed her fingertips to the side window, then to her cheek, hoping the cold would calm the blush she could feel rising to her face.

As much as she didn't want to admit it, on the surface Caden was right in so many of his assessments of her mother. But what he didn't see was that Maureen never went into a relationship with malicious intent. At least, not as far as Lucy had ever been able to tell. Her mother always seemed to believe she was head over heels in love with whatever man she'd set her cap for in the moment. Unfortunately, that didn't make Maureen's romantic history appear any less dubious.

"Are you a Crimson native?" she asked, needing to fill the silence between them and distract Caden from whatever thoughts he was having about Maureen. Lucy could tell by the set of his jaw that they weren't positive.

He gave a brief shake of his head. "I moved here when I was ten."

"To live with Garrett?"

"I was with a foster family after my mom died."

"I'm sorry."

One big shoulder lifted. "It's not a big deal. She wasn't much of a mother, anyway."

Barely slowing, he turned off the highway and down the long gravel drive that led to Sharpe Ranch. Lucy grabbed hold of the door handle when the truck's tires slid on the snow-covered road. Clearly Caden was more affected by his mom's death than he professed to be.

Lucy wanted to push him for more, intensely curious as to the circumstances that had made him Garrett Sharpe's son. As a girl, she'd entertained embarrassing fantasies about being adopted by a wholesome, all-American, network-sitcom-type family. A family where the mom baked batches of homemade cookies instead of spending hours dolling herself up for whatever man she was trying to impress that week.

Guilt lingered over the daydreams that had made her feel disloyal to her mom. In her own needy and immature way, Maureen loved Lucy to distraction. But Lucy had always wondered what it would have been like to get a do-over on her tiny dysfunctional family.

Caden had been given that gift, but she guessed it had come at a steep price. Besides, it was dangerous to know him better. Her feelings for him were already a jumble when she needed to stay clear as to her purpose at the ranch. The task her mother had given her.

She couldn't fall for him and still do her job as Maureen's faithful lackey. And even though she hated that role, it felt as much a part of her as her own skin.

He pulled to a stop in front of the main house. The porch light glowed in the dark and snow swirled around her as she climbed out of the truck. The air felt even colder now that she'd warmed up a bit, but she couldn't stop herself from lifting her face and catching a few icy flakes in her open mouth.

She opened her eyes to find Caden standing directly in front of her. "Snow tastes like a fluffy winter cloud," she said, feeling like she owed him an explanation for her behavior.

A layer of white dusted the brim of his Stetson and his wide shoulders. He didn't seem to notice the frigid temperature at all, even though he wore only a thin navy-striped Western shirt tucked into his dark jeans.

Lucy'd met a lot of men in her life, but this surly rancher was her first bona fide cowboy. She'd never fancied herself a fan of the John Wayne/Clint Eastwood cliché, but the butterflies dancing across her stomach as Caden's eyes darkened in the soft light told a different story.

Apparently she had a thing for cowboys.

That generalization was easier to swallow than admitting the low hum of lust buzzing through her was a response only to Caden.

"You're an odd one," he said quietly, but his mouth curved into a slow smile, making the words feel like a strange sort of compliment.

"One of a kind," she agreed, trying to make her tone sunny. "That's me."

He gave a slight shake of his head. "I don't want you here."

The desire whirling through her deflated like a day-old helium balloon. "Well, that's just too bad for you, then." She made to move past him, but he grabbed her arms.

"But I do want you," he whispered. Before she could react to that revelation, he lowered his head and claimed her mouth.

Despite the gruffness of his tone, the kiss was shockingly gentle. A hopeful exploration. A question that she was happy to answer with a resounding yes.

His mouth was soft against hers and need shot through her, hot and sharp like a match set to her skin. The tiny part of her that wasn't lost in the moment did a little jig at knowing she wasn't the only one unable to douse the spark that flickered between them.

She swayed closer, feeling his grip tighten on her arms. It was as if he was trying to resist pulling her tight against him, and the truth of that was like a face-first fall into a snowbank.

Of course he was resisting. He'd just said he didn't want her here. Lucy knew all too well that lust wasn't a dependable emotion. It could be used to manipulate someone far too easily. Carelessly.

After a few too many painful lessons dealt by life, she'd promised herself never again to be careless with her body or her heart.

She broke away, stumbled back a few steps and raised her hand to her mouth. The still-falling snow-flakes seemed to sizzle against her heated skin. "And you were worried about Chad taking advantage of me?" she accused. "Pot, meet Kettle."

Caden took off his hat and slapped it against one thigh, ran a hand through his hair. "I'm not…"

"No," she interrupted. "I'm not going to let you hurt me or whatever else you think is within your power. And I'm sure as hell not going to let you chase me away."

He laughed harshly. "Is that what it felt like I was doing?"

"Good night, Caden," she said instead of answering. "Thanks for the ride."

Then she turned and rushed toward the house.

Chapter Five

Caden climbed the steps to the main house the following afternoon, massaging his knuckles against his aching back.

He'd slept on the lumpy sofa in the barn's office the previous night, a kitten nestled against his hip while another purred contentedly on his chest. It had been cold and uncomfortable, with only a horse blanket as a cover, but he'd figured it was better than following Lucy into the house.

Not when his need for her had burned away what he believed about her motives for being in Colorado to a pile of useless ashes around his feet. There was something about the woman he couldn't seem to resist. It went beyond her physical beauty, although that was lethal in and of itself.

He couldn't deny the immediate connection he'd felt to her. As much as he wanted to sever it, the more time he spent with her, the stronger it became. Having her smile up at him as she caught snowflakes in her mouth, perfectly enjoying the quiet moment, had made his heart ache with longing to feel that kind of simple joy. So he'd kissed her. He'd tried to claim some of that pleasure through fusing his mouth to hers.

Damn if it hadn't worked, too. As soon as his lips grazed hers, a feeling of euphoria had rocketed through him like he'd just taken a hit off some kind of crazy, powerful drug. It wouldn't take much for him to become addicted to the feel of Lucy in his arms, and he realized he owed her a debt of thanks for pulling away before he forgot himself and let things go too far.

The one other time Caden had let his heart lead him with a woman, he'd ended up destroying his relationship with his brother. And Tyson had ended up dead as a result.

For that and so many other reasons, Caden needed to stay as far away from Lucy as possible.

He found an old jacket in the barn to wear for morning chores and grabbed a granola bar from the tiny kitchen in the bunkhouse. Chad pulled up just as Caden was heading toward the barn to feed and water the animals. The young ranch hand was still wearing the same clothes from the night before and sporting a quarter-sized hickey on the side of his neck. He looked like the cat that swallowed the proverbial sexual canary.

Caden wanted to punch him.

"I'm in love," Chad proclaimed at the top of his lungs, doing a few fancy dance moves as he caught up with Caden.

Caden's gaze strayed to the second floor of his father's house—to the room where he guessed Lucy was still fast asleep in the wee morning hours.

"Keep your voice down."

Chad lightly punched him in the arm. "You and Luce have a late night?"

"No, but you shouldn't have left her stranded at Elevation."

"I didn't strand her," Chad argued. "I saw you come in and knew you'd take care of her."

"She's not my responsibility."

Chad laughed. "You make everyone your responsibility, boss. Want to hear about my night with Jessica?"

"Hell, no."

Chad told him anyway, peppering in enough sappy details to make the granola bar he'd eaten threaten to make a repeat appearance. He'd finally managed to shut the kid up by sending him out to the far pasture to make sure the cattle had enough food and water.

Caden kept himself busy the rest of the morning and did his best to pretend he wasn't regularly checking for activity in the house.

Despite her claim that he wasn't going to chase her away, he'd half expected Lucy to pack up her compact rental car and take off for town. And as much as that would have simplified his life, he feared it would have also been a big disappointment.

He liked the way she stood up to him. He was accustomed to intimidating people with his size and silence and was a master at using both as an excuse to maintain his solitary lifestyle.

But after only a day and a half, Lucy's presence on the ranch suited him in some strange way. Garrett had always warned him that being alone and being lonely were two distinct beasts. For the first time, Caden understood the message his dad was trying to convey.

Which was why he'd decided to take his lunch break in the main house. He could scrounge together a meal from the bunkhouse kitchen, but he could no longer resist the urge to check in on Lucy. Part of him hoped he'd find her lounging on the sofa reading a gossip magazine or doing her nails or whatever gold-digger daughters did when they were trying to pass the time.

Instead, as he walked into the house, the distinct smell of lemons and oil soap hit him. The cherry table that sat in the entry, the one that Tyson had told him came from his grandmother's house in Kansas, gleamed in a way Caden had never seen before.

When Tyson and Caden were young, Garrett had hired a local woman to be at the house when they came home from school and he was out working. She made simple meals and did some light cleaning but had quickly tired of the two Sharpe boys' antics and quit.

Garrett had immediately put both Tyson and Caden to work, giving them enough chores around the ranch to keep them exhausted and out of mischief. Caden still found plenty of trouble, despite Tyson's efforts to keep him on a straight path. Garrett hired a housecleaning service to come through once a month, so even with three men living on the ranch, it was never too disgusting. Now Caden realized how much they'd been missing all those years without a woman's touch.

He was even more shocked as he stepped into the living room to see Lucy balancing precariously on a kitchen chair that she'd pulled up to the edge of the brick fireplace surround. She was reaching out to place a string of holly across the picture hanging above the mantel.

The chair had two legs on the ground and two on the higher brick and teetered back and forth as she stretched forward. A sudden vision of Lucy crashing her head on the brick had his heart pounding.

"What the hell are you doing?" he bellowed as he rushed toward her.

Apparently yelling was the exact way to make his vision a reality. She gasped, then turned to him. As the chair rocked, she tumbled backward with a yelp.

Caden caught her before she landed, his heart racing as he hugged her tight to his chest. Immediately she squirmed in his arms and he set her away from him.

"Are you trying to kill me?" she demanded as soon as her feet hit the floor.

"Why would I need to when you were doing a fine job of it yourself?"

She shook the strand of holly in his direction. "I had everything under control until you scared the pants off me."

"Hardly," he muttered, taking in the fitted jeans that hugged her curves. She wore a flowing, flower-patterned blouse over them and her feet were bare. He took in the bright pink polish on her toes and his gut reaction felt akin to a matador waving a red flag in front of an angry bull.

He pointed to her feet. "You're not wearing shoes."

"Thanks for the news flash, Captain Obvious."

"It's the middle of December."

"I'm in the house." She threw up her hands. "I don't like wearing shoes in the house."

"You should put on socks." He raked a hand through his hair. "Or slippers. Something."

"Are my feet so offensive to you?"

He almost laughed at the absurdity of the question. On the contrary, her bare feet were some sort of peculiar, diabolical temptation. They made him want to see the rest of her body. To lay her across his bed and peel off her clothes until every inch of her was exposed for his eyes only.

Coupled with the way his body had roared to life just by holding her for a few seconds—her soft curves pressed to him—Caden was reminded why he'd slept in the barn last night.

"The chair was tipping," he muttered instead of answering her question. "You were going to fall."

She stared at him for a few moments, then let out a breath. "Hold it for me while I hang the holly."

Without waiting for a response, she climbed onto the chair once more, and Caden gripped the top rail to keep it steady. Unfortunately, that put him at eye level with her perfectly rounded back end, and he forced his gaze away from her.

He didn't understand why Lucy made him feel like a randy teenager instead of a full-grown man in control of his faculties. There was no control around her.

So instead he focused his attention on the rest of the room. The gaudy, over-the-top Christmas trimmings Maureen had strewed across every surface had been replaced with Julia Sharpe's understated—and in many cases homemade—holiday decorations.

The bubble of happiness that rose in him, light and luminous, was a surprise. Something about seeing the house decked out in the Christmas finery he'd come to love over the years gave him a feeling of deep satisfaction. Caden would have never described himself as the sentimental type, and yet...

He took in the little folk Santas and the snowman candles that cheerily decorated the bookshelves. Across the back of the upright piano, Lucy had spread a quilted runner in checkered patterns of red and gold. She'd arranged the ceramic nativity scene that had always been Garrett's pride and joy on top.

"You can change it if that's not where it goes," Lucy said softly. He jerked his head around and realized she'd finished with the holly and was standing next to the chair in front of him. "I know families have certain traditions about decorating. The nativity set looked right there to me, but—"

"It's right," he interrupted. "That's where my dad always put it."

She walked over to the piano and picked up one of the ceramic sheep. "I love how it's painted. The details and color for each figure are perfect."

"Julia painted it the Christmas before she was diagnosed with cancer."

Lucy lifted her gaze to his, her whiskey-colored eyes gentle. "Julia was Garrett's wife?"

He nodded. "She died a couple of months before I met Tyson. That's why the counselor made him be my tour guide when I first came to Crimson Elementary. She thought we'd have something in common because neither of us had moms."

"That's a tragic common denominator," Lucy whispered.

"Our situations were totally different, anyway. From everything I ever learned about Julia Sharpe, she was the perfect mother. The exact opposite of mine." He moved forward and took the figure from her hand, returning it to its place on the back of the piano. "My first Christmas on the ranch, I was screwing around with the nativity scene and broke off the donkey's ear."

He ran a finger along the barely visible seam where Garrett had glued the animal back together. "I did a lot of stupid things when I was younger, especially when I was trying to test Garrett and see what it would take to make him send me away. But I've never seen him as angry as he was in that moment."

"Do you really think he would have sent you away once he claimed you?"

He stilled and fisted his hand at his side. How could he admit that she'd just voiced his most secret fear? The one he couldn't quite release?

Even after everything they'd been through and the love and devotion Garrett had shown him, Caden was still waiting for the day it all ended. He wondered if he'd ever be able to trust himself not to ruin the good things in his life.

"Your mother isn't going to be happy that you took down her Pepto-Bismol-colored winter wonderland in here."

She shrugged. "My mom means well, but Christmas is about tradition." She laughed, as if surprised to hear those words out of her own mouth. "At least, that's what I'm told."

"You didn't have traditions?" As much as he didn't want to be curious about this woman, he couldn't help wanting to know more about her.

"Not really. Nothing lasting."

"Sort of like your mother's three marriages," he blurted before thinking about it.

He regretted the words immediately. Lucy's gaze hardened and her full lips pressed into a thin line. She went to move past him, but he placed a hand on her arm.

"I'm sorry, Lucy."

"I doubt that."

"It's the truth." He bent his knees so he was at eye level with her. "I appreciate what you did in here."

"I meant it as an olive branch," she said, her gaze steady on his. "I'm not the enemy, Caden."

He toyed with the idea of that for a moment and found that it felt right. True. "I know."

"And neither is my mom," she added.

He couldn't allow himself to believe that but didn't argue. For once in his damn life, he was tired of arguing.

"We need a tree," he told her, gesturing to the box of ornaments still shoved in the corner. "There's enough time to head up into the forest and get one now."

"I thought you and your dad were going tree hunting when he got back."

"He won't mind if we take care of it." Actually, Garrett would probably be thrilled if Caden and Lucy dealt with hauling a tree back from the forest surrounding the ranch. The old man had seemed to age decades since Tyson's death. He could no longer spend long days working the ranch. After a few hours on horseback checking the fence line, Caden would often find that his father had retreated back to the house and his comfy chair in front of the fire.

It was difficult to know whether time or grief was the hardest on Garrett, but Caden imagined his father would appreciate a reprieve from their annual trip into the forest to cut down a tree.

She crossed her arms over her chest and studied him before answering. "I can't decide if you're extending your own olive branch or trying to lure me into the woods to have some kind of high-altitude Tony Soprano moment."

Caden felt his mouth kick up and found it odd that even when she was challenging him, Lucy could make him smile more than he had in years. "Let's call it an olive branch." He lifted a brow. "For now, anyway."

She laughed, as he'd hoped she would. "I'll get ready."

"Meet me out front in twenty minutes," he told her, then cleared her throat. "Unless you need more time?" When he'd been with Becca, she'd taken close to an hour to get ready no matter what they had planned for the day. It still blew his mind that once upon a time he'd fallen for such a high-maintenance woman. And it made his stomach clench that he hadn't realized the twisted game she was playing with him and his brother until it was too late.

Lucy only shook her head. "I just need to find warmer clothes. It won't take long."

He nodded, and she left the room. He waited until she was up the stairs before he blew out a breath. An olive branch or rope to string up his heart once again?

It was difficult to know exactly what he was offering when Lucy had his emotions so jumbled.

Fifteen minutes later, Lucy walked out onto the front porch. She shielded her eyes from the sun reflecting off the snow that blanketed the ground. Although the air was cold, the sky was a swath of brilliant blue as far as she could see.

The white-capped peak of Crimson Mountain loomed in the distance, like a benevolent ruler presiding over its kingdom.

"I definitely won't lose you in that coat," Caden called from where he stood in the gravel driveway.

Lucy smoothed a hand over the down jacket she'd found in her mother's closet, the hue a shade of pink that seemed more appropriate for Miami Beach than the Colorado mountains.

"It's the warmest thing I could find," she answered and pulled the coordinating knit cap farther down around her ears.

She'd put on athletic leggings under her jeans to act as another layer of warmth and tucked her jeans into a pair of fleece-lined snow boots.

She'd told herself it didn't matter how she looked because she wasn't trying to impress Caden. Of course, that hadn't stopped her from applying a fresh coat of gloss on her mouth. But only so her lips wouldn't chap.

Not because she wanted Caden to notice them. Not because she couldn't stop thinking about his mouth on hers the previous night.

But if she had been thinking about the kiss they'd shared, she'd have to admit she'd never felt anything like it. Lucy couldn't remember ever responding to a man the way she had to Caden. The featherlight touch of his mouth had made her body zip to life like some kind of fancy race car with the pedal slammed to the floor. Then he'd deepened the kiss and the rush of desire made her feel as if she was hurtling over a cliff with no parachute.

At that moment she would have done anything he asked. She wanted everything he was willing to give, which scared the hell out of her. Wanting made her weak. Needing something she wasn't meant to have was a sure path to heartache.

Only her finely tuned self-preservation skills had forced her to break away and retreat to the house. She'd lain in bed in the small guest room she occupied, waiting to hear his footsteps on the stairs, her body still humming with desire even as she recited in her head all the reasons Caden was bad news for her.

But when she'd awakened in the morning, early enough to watch the sky beginning to turn from gray to orange, something had pulled her out of bed and to the window just in time to see Caden walking from the barn, still wearing the same clothes as the night before.

Apparently she wasn't the only one who realized how dangerous their connection could prove to be. She'd made coffee and a bowl of oatmeal, hurrying in case he made a morning appearance to get his own breakfast, but the house had remained quiet.

After a shower, she'd slipped into the chair behind Garrett's oversize cherry desk in the second-floor office and powered up the computer. She'd spent the next couple of hours poring over ledgers and spreadsheets, increasingly baffled as to the ranch's financial records.

She'd gotten her associate's degree taking evening classes over a three-year span of time and had kept the books for the high-end boutique where she'd worked in Florida. Secretly she dreamed of going back to school for a full-fledged business degree, although how she'd find the time or the money to make that a reality wasn't clear.

But while she'd always had a knack for numbers, the Sharpe Ranch books made her feel like a second grader struggling with the fundamentals of adding and subtracting. There were several spreadsheets dealing with day-to-day ranch operations, expenditures and income from hay and grain. Then she found the accounting records that covered Garrett's other holdings, from business investments to a few high-level land development deals around Crimson.

Although some of the entries were recent, it was difficult to tell if the books seemed so convoluted because of her unfamiliarity with ranching business or because the record keeping had been ignored or mismanaged since Tyson's death.

Eventually she'd walked away from the computer, wandering to the window to gaze at the lone figure on horseback far out in the pasture. Her attraction to Caden made her feel like a lovesick schoolgirl, so she'd pushed away from the window and made her way downstairs, hoping to find something to distract her from thoughts of the handsome rancher.

Which was what had led her to switching out her mother's tacky holiday decorations for the ones that clearly belonged in the cozy farmhouse. Normally Lucy didn't mess with Christmas. She'd worked retail since she was sixteen, which meant she'd seen the best and the worst of the holiday spirit. She also knew the words to every corny seasonal song ever written and had put up and taken down more plastic trees than she cared to count.

But she'd long ago given up hope of being the recipient of any Christmas miracles. The holiday season was for working—waiting on impatient customers and helping others choose the perfect gifts for friends and loved ones while she preferred to spend her Christmas watching old movies and eating take-out Chinese from the carton.

Yet here she was walking toward Caden and what looked like the mountain version of a golf cart with a metal trailer hooked to the back. And those damn butterflies went crazy once more, both at the sight of Caden in his fitted jeans and Stetson and the thought of an adventure in the woods.

"You'll appreciate the warmth when we get going," he said, moving aside and opening the vehicle's door for her. "It's a perfect day and the UTV has heat but since the top's open, the wind can get chilly when the sun starts to set."

"UTV?" She arched a brow. "That sounds like something I'd make a doctor's appointment to handle."

Caden chuckled and shook his head. "Utility terrain vehicle," he explained. "The path into the forest is too narrow for the truck."

"Got it." She climbed in and immediately the heat from the vents under the dashboard warmed her feet. A moment later Caden spread a heavy blanket over her legs. Lucy resisted the urge to sigh as he tucked it firmly under her thighs.

"It's no fun out there if you're half-frozen," he told her.

"Thanks," she whispered. She tried to ignore the scent of him, shampoo and spearmint gum, even as it tangled through her senses. He hadn't mentioned the kiss or shown any sign that he even remembered pulling her into his arms. Maybe he'd stayed away from the house last night because he'd feared she'd try to seduce him.

He'd made no secret of the fact that he believed her mom to be a gold digger and Lucy to be cut from the same cloth.

She had to keep that in mind. Her mother wanted her to convince Caden that having Maureen as a stepmom was a good thing. That was Lucy's only purpose in Colorado. It definitely wasn't in anyone's best interest to lose a piece of her heart to this man.

Caden threw her a sidelong glance as he climbed behind the wheel. "Everything okay?"

"Yep. Let's find a Christmas tree."

Caden looked like he wanted to call her out on her lie, but instead he shifted the UTV and they rumbled out of the driveway and down the snow-packed trail that led toward the forest.

Lucy had never been one for nature outings. A chair on the beach and her toes in the water were about as adventurous as she got. But riding in the off-road vehicle was exhilarating. They raced across the landscape, bumping slightly as the trail dipped and pitched. Soon they were in the trees, and her breath caught at the beauty surrounding her.

The pine tree needles were laced with snow, and icicles hung suspended from some of the longer branches. The forest was dappled in sunlight, although she definitely felt a drop in temperature as they made their way up the trail and left the open fields behind them.

Caden seemed to know the area well and maneuvered the UTV around corners and across a frozen creek bed. The trail grew narrow in some spots and Lucy laughed as the roll bar on the UTV brushed a low-hanging branch and they were dusted with snow.

Eventually they drove into a clearing, and Caden abruptly cut the engine.

"What's wrong?" she asked, grabbing his arm. Although there was no doubt Caden knew his way around the forest, the city girl in her didn't like the thought of being stuck out in the woods in the middle of December.

Caden leaned close and used one finger to turn her head to the side. "Look over there," he whispered, pointing with his other hand to the far edge of the meadow.

Lucy's breath caught in her throat as her gaze tracked to the massive animal staring at her through big black eyes. "Reindeer," she whispered.

Caden's soft chuckle was warm against her jaw. "Elk," he corrected her. "You know the herd bull because he has the antlers. Six points."

The elk's antlers were massive but she had no experience with wildlife in the...well...the wild. "Unless you're talking basketball, six points means nothing to me."

"Count the tips sticking out on each antler. He's called a six by six."

"And the rest are girls?"

"Cows," Caden clarified.

"Does that one bull service all the ladies?"

Caden laughed again. "Yeah. During the spring and summer, the cows and young elk are often on their own. But there are usually one or two bulls with the herd through the winter."

"So he's a busy guy."

"I doubt it's a problem for him."

Lucy couldn't help but smile. "Right."

The elk made a noise and the females who were nosing in the snow looked up. A few pawed at the ground and snuffled. Then the herd moved forward and disappeared into the trees.

"That was amazing." Lucy turned to Caden, surprised to find that he hadn't moved away from her. Her nose grazed his cheek and he sat back like she'd burned him. "I didn't realize elk were so beautiful."

"They're majestic," he agreed. "That herd stays on the ranch most of the year."

She looked around. "Is this still your property? I thought we were on public land here."

"A few miles up the trail it becomes forest-service land," he told her, pointing to the other side of the clearing. "Garrett has almost two thousand acres. He inherited a lot from his dad but has added acreage as land became available over the years."

"You don't work the whole thing, do you?"

"A lot of it is natural prairie or forest. The cattle are free-range so in the summer they spread out pretty far. But Crimson has grown quite a bit even since I was a kid. Garrett wants to make sure some of the open spaces are preserved."

"You do that a lot," she murmured.

He cocked a brow.

"You refer to him as Garrett and not Dad."

A muscle ticked in Caden's jaw. "He's my dad."

"I know that." But she got the distinct impression that Caden didn't quite believe it even after almost twenty years of living on the ranch.

"Let's find a tree before the weather turns."

"What are you talking about?" Lucy pointed a finger toward the sky. "It's a perfect day."

"There were storm clouds gathering on the peak as we left the ranch. They should get to us within the hour."

"Um…okay." Lucy had always gotten her weather forecasts from the local news, but she wasn't going to argue. Instead, she hopped out of the UTV. "What tree do you want?"

"Whichever one makes you happy." Caden pulled an ax from the trailer and came to stand next to her.

She crossed her arms over her chest. "I can't pick. I don't know what makes a good Christmas tree."

He gave her an incredulous look. "You've celebrated Christmas before, right?"

"Well, yes. But never with a real tree. Or even a fake one that's full-size." She tugged on the hem of her pink parka. "Except at some of the stores where I worked. But I didn't pay much attention as we were putting them up."

"You've never had a real tree?"

She waved a hand in the air. "Too much trouble."

"Not even when you were a kid?"

"Definitely not," she admitted. "My mom didn't like the mess of pine needles on the carpet."

He studied her for a moment as if weighing an important decision. Then he handed her the small ax he held. "Let's go find the biggest, most beautiful Christmas tree that will fit in the house. We have a lot of years to make up for."

Without waiting for an answer, he turned and started into the forest. Lucy stared after him, blinking away unbidden tears. She'd told herself for so many years that there was no such thing as Christmas spirit—it was just a materialistic holiday that produced fake cheer and the need for people to spend money they didn't have.

Although working retail did that to a person, even before endless hours spent at a cash register, she'd given up on Christmas. Year after year of having her mom care about the holiday only when there was a man around to impress had worn on Lucy. Some years there was an abundance of over-the-top gifts and some years, when depression had its claws dug deep, Maureen could barely rouse herself out of bed. Lucy didn't trust Christmas. It had shown itself to be a fickle friend.

The idea that Caden wanted to make up for that overwhelmed her. She hadn't even admitted to him her pathetic history, yet he still knew just what to do to give her the happiest holiday moment she could remember.

Maybe it was silly, but the thought of a real Christmas tree made Lucy feel like a little girl again. Anticipation bubbled up inside her and she didn't bother to tamp it down. This afternoon had nothing to do with her mother or convincing Caden that the marriage was a good idea.

This moment was all about Lucy's happiness. It was long past time she made herself a priority in her own life.

Caden paused and looked over his shoulder. "Are we doing this?"

She quickly swiped at her eyes and held up the ax. "Call me Paula Bunyan," she said and hurried to join him.

Chapter Six

Lucy stopped so suddenly that Caden almost ran into her. "That's it," she whispered.

He followed her line of sight and frowned. "What's it?"

"The perfect Christmas tree." She moved forward awkwardly, her boots crunching as she sank into the snow.

They'd been walking through the woods for almost forty-five minutes. As Caden predicted, clouds had rolled in and the temperature had dropped. Snow flurries whirled through the air, and Caden was slowly losing sensation in his toes. He hadn't realized how long the outing would take and regretted not wearing insulated boots.

Despite her years as a Floridian, Lucy seemed strangely undeterred by the cold or snow or waning daylight. It was like he'd unleashed a kid in a Christmas tree candy store. She'd vetoed at least a dozen beautiful trees that would have fit perfectly on Sharpe Ranch. But the one she was proudly standing in front of now...

"Are you going for the *A Charlie Brown Christmas* look?" he asked, rubbing his gloved hands together.

"This is a beautiful tree," she argued. "Not too big and not too small."

"You sure about that, Goldilocks? It looks a little scraggly from where I'm standing."

She rolled her eyes and turned to the tree, holding up her palms to each side of the branches like she was covering its ears. "Don't listen to him. I see your potential. You are perfect just the way you are."

The words were like a fist to Caden's gut. They were eerily similar to what Garrett had said when he'd first spoken to him about adoption. Ironically, the conversation had taken place after Caden purposely knocked over a big bag of horse feed in the barn. Garrett had sent Tyson to the house and ordered Caden to sit down on a bale of hay so they could "talk."

From what Caden had then deduced from both his mother and his more recent foster parents, on good days a "talk" meant the back side of an adult's hand or on bad days, the sharp sting of a belt on his bare skin. Instead Garrett had reached behind the hay bale and picked up a squirming kitten from the litter the resident barn cat had given birth to weeks before.

He'd dropped the ball of fluff into Caden's arms and waited. Caden had tried to stay still and withhold any emotion, but the sweet kitten was too much—even for a surly kid. He'd lifted the kitten and cuddled it to his chest, all the while muttering about how much the animal annoyed him.

Garrett had smiled and said, "You've got potential." Then he'd asked Caden how he'd feel about coming to live on Sharpe Ranch permanently.

Sometimes Caden wondered if he'd ever live up to the potential his adoptive father had first seen in him.

"Let's bring it home, then," he told Lucy now.

"Really?" Her cheeks were pink from either cold or excitement. He couldn't tell which. Snowflakes clung to her gaudy pink hat, and her hair looked even darker as she swung it over her shoulder. "I thought you didn't like this one."

"It's your tree. Plus I'm freezing. I want to get the hell out of the woods."

"Come on, baby," she crooned to the tree, and unwanted heat pooled in Caden's belly at her voice's sultry cadence. "You're mine now."

It was a miracle Caden's tongue didn't loll out of his mouth. For a moment he suspected she was talking to the tree in that tone just to mess with him. Then she lifted the ax and waved it around with so much disregard for her own safety that he forgot all his lustful thoughts and concentrated on keeping her from chopping off her own head.

"This isn't *The Walking Dead*," he warned. "You don't have to mutilate it." He strode forward and turned her so her back was to him. "I'll show you." He adjusted her grip on the ax and demonstrated the proper technique for felling a tree.

The Douglas fir was barely taller than a shrub. He watched as she bent low and swung forward, the ax's sharp blade thunking into the trunk.

"You do the rest," she said, leaving the ax stuck in the tree. "I feel like I'm hurting him."

He gave her a long look. "It's a tree."

"Trees are living things," she countered.

"Right." He'd never met anyone like Lucy, a mind-boggling blend of sophistication and innocence. But despite his frozen toes, Caden couldn't remember the last time he'd had so much fun.

He pulled the ax from the tree and chopped it down with several well-placed swings. The good thing about Lucy's scraggly tree was that the size made it easy to haul back to the UTV. Although they'd walked through the woods longer than he expected, Lucy had actually circled back toward the main path, so it didn't take long to reach the vehicle.

"The snow is really coming down," Lucy said as he hefted the tree into the trailer.

"We're supposed to get six inches overnight."

He turned on the UTV and climbed in next to Lucy. The blanket covered her lap, but he could see the shivers passing through her.

She turned to him and made a face. "I didn't notice the cold when I was searching for the perfect tree, but now…"

"Come here," he told her, and she scooted toward him on the bench seat. She smelled like flowery shampoo and the cold, and he wrapped an arm around her waist, pulling her even closer. His body tightened when she snuggled against him.

The ride back to the ranch was slower than he would have liked with visibility lowered because of the blowing snow.

He finally pulled to a stop in front of the house and turned to Lucy. "I'll bring in the tree, and then I need to check on the animals in the barn. You should go inside and warm up."

"Do you need help?" she asked through chattering teeth.

"I need you to not turn into a Popsicle on my watch," he answered and pulled the blanket from around her.

"I think I can manage that." She got out of the UTV and walked up the porch steps and into the house.

He got the tree onto the porch and dusted it off, then covered it with the tarp he had in the UTV's trailer. He headed to the barn next and made sure all of his animals were warm and dry.

Chad came in just as Caden was about to head to the house. "There's a problem with the propane heater near the trough in the west pasture."

Caden cursed under his breath. With the temperatures dropping and snow in the forecast, he couldn't afford for the herd's drinking water to freeze.

"I need to put on my other boots and I'll be ready to go."

Chad eyed his feet then raised a brow. "You're liable to lose a toe to frostbite wearing those in this weather."

"Don't be a drama queen," Caden muttered. "I'm fine. I didn't expect to be out so long."

"I saw you and Lucy heading for the woods earlier. Hot date?"

"No date at all. We went to get a Christmas tree."

"How romantic," Chad said in a singsong voice.

"Shut it," Caden told him.

"It's okay to admit you're human," Chad shot back. "Any man with two eyes and half a heartbeat would be into her. She's hot as hell. I mean, if Jessica and I don't work out, I could give you some competition."

Caden leveled a look at his young ranch hand. "Lucy is off-limits for you."

He expected an argument or some kind of smart comeback, but Chad only grinned. "I figured as much."

Caden finished pulling on his heavy work boots and stood. "Let's take care of the heater before we lose all our daylight."

It was almost six that evening when Lucy heard the front door open and shut. She pushed away from the computer where she'd been working for the past hour and ran a hand through her hair.

She didn't want to admit, even to herself, that her feelings were hurt because Caden had ditched her at the house with the Christmas tree. It had been foolish to read so much into their jaunt to the forest.

She wanted it to mean something that he'd suggested she pick out the Christmas tree for the house. Clearly, all it meant was that he didn't want to be bothered with the task.

As cold as she'd been on the ride home, it had felt amazing to press herself against Caden's strong body, the heat of him warming her. It embarrassed her now that she'd run into the house and changed into her best jeans and a red V-neck sweater, spritzing herself with perfume as she anticipated a late afternoon spent trimming the tree and cuddling in front of the fire.

She'd even made hot cocoa, which had long ago cooled in the pan on the stove. She'd finally realized he wasn't coming back to the house. Her stupid little fantasy about a picture-perfect holiday moment was just that. A fantasy. She should have known better. It's why Lucy didn't like Christmas to begin with—as soon as she allowed herself to have holiday expectations, she was disappointed when things didn't work out the way she wanted.

Just to prove that she wasn't waiting for him, she'd dragged the tree into the house, leaving a trail of pine needles in her wake. She'd found a tree stand in the bottom of one of the ornament boxes and managed to get the tree upright in one corner of the living room. Who needed a man, anyway?

Maybe Caden had been right about the size. It looked a little scraggly now that it wasn't surrounded by other trees, but she still loved it. Even though it had been cut down on Sharpe Ranch property and now stood in Garrett's house, the tree belonged to Lucy.

And she hadn't waited to decorate it because she was still hoping Caden would show up. Nope. She'd just wanted to put in some more time on the financials before she had her own private tree-trimming party.

She quickly turned back to the computer when footsteps sounded on the stairs. Let him come to her, and she could blow him off just as easily.

"Hey, there."

She glanced up and pretended to be surprised to see him standing in the doorway, as if she'd been so engrossed in her work she hadn't heard him come in. She most certainly hadn't been waiting for him.

"Oh, hello," she said breezily, like she was greeting a casual acquaintance she hadn't seen in months. "I lost track of time. Did you have a nice afternoon?"

He reached out to grip either side of the door frame with his hands, making him look even broader than normal. He'd taken off his hat and his hair was rumpled and sticking up in several places, as if he'd been raking his hands through it. He still wore his heavy canvas jacket and his cheeks were bright pink, his eyes tired.

"No," he told her, moving toward the desk, "my afternoon sucked." He pressed his knuckles against the cherry top and leaned forward, the scent of winter and ranch work spilling off him. "I'd thought I was going to spend it with you, and instead I've been dealing with an emergency with one of the propane heaters."

"Oh," she breathed as relief rushed through her. He hadn't ditched her after all. There'd been a ranch emergency. He definitely looked exhausted and unhappy.

"You could have told me," she blurted even though he didn't owe her an explanation. He didn't owe her anything. But her feelings had been bruised, and it was hard to let that go.

He straightened, and she thought he might walk away. "You did good getting the tree in on your own. I would have helped."

"I wasn't sure you were coming back."

"I'm sorry," he said quietly.

She shrugged. "This is stupid. You don't want to hang out with me. You don't even want me on the ranch. It's silly for us to try to be friends."

"Friends," he repeated, chewing on the word like it was something he'd never tasted before. "Are we friends, Lucy?"

"You tell me, Caden."

"I'd like to be your friend," he admitted after a moment, "but that doesn't change how I feel about your mother."

"Maybe we should leave my mom and your dad out of this," she suggested. "At least for a little while."

"Good idea." One side of his mouth quirked. "An even better idea would be a shower."

Lucy felt her mouth drop open, as those darned butterflies did their thing in her belly.

Caden chuckled. "Me in the shower," he clarified. "Alone."

She blew out a breath. "I knew that."

His slow grin widened. "I need to wash off this day and after that, I'd like to eat dinner and decorate the tree." He arched a brow. "The dinner and decorating part with you." He frowned when she didn't answer. "If you don't have other plans?"

She barked out a laugh. "No plans. But I don't cook."

"I do," he told her. "Give me ten minutes."

"You can shower and get changed in ten minutes?" Lucy wasn't high maintenance, but that seemed lightning fast.

"Want to watch?" he asked.

She felt color flood her cheeks. "Of course not."

"Liar," he whispered and walked out of the room.

She thought about throwing the stapler at his head, but the thought of someone cooking dinner for her was too appealing. Maureen was a fabulous cook, but she chose to use her culinary skills only when a man was involved. When her mother was in a relationship, they ate like kings.

But when it was just the two of them, Lucy had become adept at heating canned spaghetti and various frozen dinners. As a result, she'd come to view cooking as another form of manipulation—a tool in her mother's arsenal for snaring whatever man she'd set her sights on in the moment.

Even when Lucy had moved out on her own, she'd refused to learn to cook. Her lack of culinary skills drove her mother crazy, and it had been a weak form of rebellion but one Lucy'd never outgrown.

When she heard the shower turn on in the hall bathroom, she jumped up from the chair and practically tripped her way down the stairs. It would be pure torture to sit there and imagine Caden stripping off his clothes and stepping under a steaming hot shower.

She'd been through plenty in her life, but torture wasn't high on her to-do list.

She stumbled toward the front door, trying hard to push the image of a naked Caden from her brain. She yanked open the door and stepped out onto the front porch, hoping the bracing air would cool the fire raging through her body.

Her breath came out in puffy clouds in front of her face, and she dug her toes into the ice-cold coir doormat.

"Everything okay, Lucy?" a deep voice called.

She glanced up to see Chad staring at her from across the driveway.

"Just enjoying December in Colorado," she shouted, giving him a wave.

He looked at her like she'd lost her mind, and maybe that was true. Never had she reacted to a man like she did to Caden. In fact, she'd always secretly judged her mother for having no willpower when it came to guys and falling so fast and hard whenever a handsome man crossed her path.

Now Lucy feared she'd inherited more from her mom than a decent complexion and a love for jelly donuts.

When Chad continued to stare, she waved again and backed into the house. She made her way to the kitchen and opened the fridge, hoping to distract herself by finding something to start for dinner. There were various containers of cheese and meat and a whole drawer full of vegetables, but to Lucy it felt like trying to read a book in a foreign language.

Finally she pulled out a head of lettuce, a yellow

bell pepper and a bag of baby carrots. At least she was fluent in salad.

She was chopping a handful of carrots when Caden walked into the room, and she promptly came close to cutting off the tip of her finger.

Usually he was handsome in his rancher gear of the ubiquitous denim shirt and Carhartt jacket, but tonight he wore a plain white T-shirt that stretched across his chest and low-slung jeans hugging his muscled legs in a way that made her mouth go dry. From under one sleeve she could just see the shadow of dark ink. Not surprising for a man like Caden, but the urge she had to trace her fingers and tongue across his skin was shocking.

She schooled her features and offered a smile she hoped came off as friendly and not predatory. The truth was that outside her outrageous desire for Caden, she actually liked him. If she discounted the fact that he pretty much despised her mother and wanted Lucy off the ranch and out of his life.

Conflicting goals when it came to their parents notwithstanding, she had fun with him. She respected his work ethic and his protective instinct when it came to Garrett.

Of course, her heart melted at what he was doing to rescue and rehome the animals in his care. He made her laugh and he got her humor. It wasn't natural for Lucy to feel comfortable hanging out with men. She'd been raised to see them as either conquests or not worth her time. But it was easy to be herself around Caden.

She figured nothing she did would change his opinion of her or her mom, but the camaraderie was a nice break from the normal anxiety she felt with guys.

So she didn't want to mess up this chance for friendship, as fleeting as it might turn out to be.

"Feel better now?" she asked casually, and he nodded.

"When I was deployed, I used to dream about long, hot showers."

"How long were you in the army?"

He opened the refrigerator and grabbed an armload of food. "I did two tours in Afghanistan and one in Iraq."

"Did you like it?"

He shrugged. "I was a decent soldier, and I liked that. It made my dad laugh how quickly I took to the routine and discipline of military life when I'd chafed against every rule he ever set for me." He was quiet for a moment as he placed the containers and bags of food on the counter. Then he added softly, "I thought I'd be a lifer."

"But you got out to help on the ranch after your brother died."

"I owed it to Garrett."

"Why?"

His sharp gaze crashed into hers. "Sorry," she said quickly. "It's none of my business."

"Tyson died while I was on leave. It was on a rock climbing trip on the other side of the pass that I was supposed to take with him. If I'd been there…" He shook his head. "He was rappelling down the last pitch of a route he knew well, but he lost sight of the end of his rope and thought it would reach the ground. He fell from about thirty feet in the air. By the time the other climbers got to him, he was gone. I would have been the strongest one in the group. I could have—"

"You can't do that," Lucy interrupted, reaching for his arm. She wrapped her fingers around his wrist and squeezed. "You weren't there. It wasn't your fault."

He stared at her hand like having someone touch his skin was unfamiliar to him. "We weren't speaking at the time," he said, his voice desperately hollow. "Tyson had moved to Denver for a job and only came back to Crimson once a month. I'd fallen hard for a woman I met on leave—a waitress here in town. Turns out she was his girlfriend, and she'd gone after me to punish him for not taking her with him when he left."

"What a bi—" Lucy stopped when Caden yanked his arm away from her.

"He tried to convince me she was using both of us, but I wouldn't listen. I accused him of being jealous because someone finally picked me over him. Things got heated and we both said things... I said things I didn't mean." He closed his eyes for a moment, and when he opened them again the stark pain in their green depths stunned Lucy.

"You loved him," she whispered. "I barely know you and I can see that in you. He knew it."

He gave a humorless laugh. "I can be a real prick when I set my mind to it."

She arched a brow. "I'm shocked."

The corners of his eyes crinkled but he didn't smile. "Tyson first brought me home when he realized my foster dad was taking out his temper on me. I know he's the one who convinced Garrett to adopt me."

"Your father is a grown man who makes his own decisions."

"Yeah, but he and Tyson were a team after Julia died. I owe everything I have to my brother, and I repaid him first by betraying him then by turning my back on him when he called me out on it."

He stepped closer, crowding her against the counter. "It wasn't a joke when I said I'd hurt you, Lucy. I ruin everything good that comes into my life."

A part of her wanted to run. As much as she tried to be tough, Lucy knew she was close to losing her heart to this man. She'd never been much of a rescuer, but something about Caden pulled at her soul. She wanted more than anything to help him heal. But she was smart enough to believe what he told her. She could very easily end up hurt.

Right now it didn't matter.

"But I'm not good for you," she said, tipping up her chin to meet his intense gaze. "Remember, I'm the enemy. That should keep me safe."

"Safe," he repeated, but his shoulders lowered slightly. "That's funny." He lifted his thumb to her mouth, traced it over the seam of her lips, then tugged down on the lower one.

Lucy forced herself not to moan at the touch. Despite his warnings and the very real risk of being hurt, she felt safe with him. He lowered his head and all she wanted was his mouth on hers. Then her stomach gave a loud rumble, breaking the spell between them.

He stepped away and moved toward the refrigerator. "You need to eat."

"What are we making?" she asked, impressed that her voice didn't shake.

He took a beer from the refrigerator and glanced over his shoulder. "Want a drink? There's beer in the fridge. Garrett has wine downstairs."

"A beer is fine."

He handed her a bottle, and she traced a finger over the blue mountains on the label.

"Chicken tacos tonight," he told her. "You've got a good start on the salad."

"How else can I help?" She twisted the cap off the beer and took a long drink. Despite the snow she could still see coming down outside the kitchen window, the cool liquid refreshed her overheated body.

"Grab the spices from the cabinet."

She laughed. "Can you be more specific? I wasn't joking when I said I don't cook."

He rattled off a list of spices and pointed to the cabinet next to the stove.

"Mind if I ask why you don't cook?" he asked as she began collecting the colorful jars on the counter. "One thing I'll say for your mom is that she knows her way around the kitchen."

Lucy's hand jerked, and a container of cumin clattered onto the counter. "She cooks to impress men," she answered honestly. "And she wanted me to learn for the same reason. It tainted cooking for me."

He gave her a small nod. "You're not your mother. You know that, right?"

"Of course," she whispered and turned back to the spice cabinet, blinking away tears. She wanted to believe that but she'd never trusted that she wouldn't turn into her mother if she weren't careful. Genetics was a powerful influencer.

They worked in mostly companionable silence for the next thirty minutes, Caden giving her only occasional directions. Soon the rich scent of spicy chicken and black beans filled the room. He showed her how to heat tortillas over the stove. Then she offered to grate a block of cheese, strangely proud to be helping with the meal.

Whenever her mom had given her tasks when cooking, it had felt like she was an indentured servant. But like everything with Caden, tonight felt new and real and like it belonged just to her.

Chapter Seven

Caden didn't understand why a simple dinner of chicken tacos eaten at the farmhouse kitchen table felt like a five-star meal, but he couldn't stop the stupid smile that curved his mouth every moment he wasn't chewing.

He'd made a thousand meals in this kitchen, but tonight was different. Lucy made it different. They cleaned up the plates and moved to the living room, her enthusiasm trickling into his bones and making him truly excited at the prospect of decorating her scrawny Christmas tree.

"We start with lights, right?" she asked, and he nodded. She pulled the strands of colored lights from one of the boxes, and they strung them around the tree, working together like they were old friends.

Friends.

Tyson had been the first friend Caden had ever had, and every day he felt the loss of his friend and brother like there was a hole in his heart. It felt wrong that this woman was quickly filling it, as if his happiness was somehow disloyal to Tyson. He'd had buddies in the army but had been remiss about staying in contact with them since he'd gotten out.

"These ornaments are so sweet," Lucy said, drawing his attention to where she knelt on the floor next to one of the boxes. She held up the wooden figures of a raccoon and deer, rough and rudimentary.

"I used to carve a new ornament for Garr—" he cleared his throat "—for my dad every year. It was the only thing he asked for each Christmas. They were pretty bad at the beginning, and I'm surprised he even trusted me with a knife."

"They deserve pride of place," she said, walking over to hang the small animals from branches at the front of the tree. The exact spot Garrett gave to his tiny creations every year. They hadn't bothered to put up a tree last year, and Caden hadn't realized how much he missed the tradition until now.

"These were from Tyson's mom," he said, handing her a box of vintage balls of all different colors. "I guess they hung on her family's tree when she was a girl. Maybe we don't mention that part to your mom."

"Maybe not," Lucy agreed as she took the box and hung the ornaments.

She looked so damn beautiful in the soft light from the Christmas tree. He continued to give her ornaments to hang, explaining the significance of each one. Pretty soon all that was left was the beaded star.

"You should do the star," she told him, crossing her arms over her chest. "I kind of took over trimming the tree."

"I liked watching you," he said honestly. Hell, he could watch her take out the trash and would probably find it fascinating.

He took the star and stretched up to place it on the top of the tree. As kids, he and Tyson had argued about who got to put the star on top until Garrett had grabbed it from their hands and announced he'd be in charge of the star every year.

"It's beautiful," she whispered when he stepped away. Her palms were pressed together and her eyes shone with delight.

"Beautiful," he repeated and moved toward her, wrapping his hand around hers and tugging her closer. He brushed his lips across hers, which he'd wanted to do all day. The tightness that had been clamped around his chest for so long loosened ever so slightly. To Caden the change felt like the slight shift of snow that could start an avalanche. He was scared as hell of being buried under the weight of it.

So when she leaned in, he pulled back, ignoring the shadow that crossed her eyes.

"I need to check on the animals one more time tonight. Thank you for a great evening."

As goodbyes went, it was pathetic. But he didn't know how to rein in his feelings for her. Without dinner to make or a tree to trim, there were no distractions. Nothing to keep him from putting his hands all over her. That was a terrible idea, even though his body shouted it would be the best way to end this evening.

"Can I help?" she asked, biting down on her bottom lip.

"It's cold and snowy out there. The barn is heated but it's not—"

"I think I can handle it," she said with a laugh, then frowned. "Unless this is you brushing me off?" She stared at him a moment. "Right. This is you brushing me off. I get it."

He shook his head. "You don't." How could he make her understand that he was trying to keep a distance between them because the alternative was that he'd want more than he should from her? More than he guessed she'd be willing to give. Keeping himself closed off was a defense mechanism he'd perfected long ago.

If he didn't care, he couldn't be hurt.

When he didn't care, he didn't hurt other people.

Lucy had already gotten under his skin, and he knew his willpower was no match for the way he wanted her.

"Then explain it to me."

"If you want to help," he said by way of an answer, "put on boots, a heavy coat and gloves. Grab a flashlight from the closet in the front hall and meet me in the barn." Then he walked past her, shoved his feet into his boots, grabbed his jacket from the hook in the entryway and headed out into the cold before he changed his mind.

He wasn't sure if she was going to follow him. He'd been purposely rude, striding to the barn like he was running away from the playground bully. Which was ridiculous and made him feel like a jerk.

He let the dogs out of their respective pens and opened the back door of the barn that led to an enclosed corral. The dogs barked and yipped, running around and doing their business, most of them oblivious to the cold. A few of the ones that were older or didn't have a heavy coat of fur went back to the barn.

As the dogs played, Caden grabbed a container of vegetables from the refrigerator in the office and let himself into the bunny room. Fritzi, the Holland Lop that was a permanent fixture in the barn and a certified therapy pet, hopped to the front of the hutch for her nightly nose rub and snack. The other rabbits followed her lead, and Caden smiled as he visited with each of them.

Once or twice he glanced over his shoulder, but when Lucy didn't appear, he figured his abrupt exit had made her want to keep her distance. He wasn't sure if he was disappointed or relieved.

Who was he fooling? It killed him to know he'd so quickly ruined his chances with a woman who made him happier than he'd been in years.

He finished with the rabbits and went to check on the cats, but a short bark from one of the dog pens had him hurrying down the barn's main corridor.

Turning the corner around the converted horse stall, he stopped in his tracks. "What are you doing?" he whispered frantically.

Lucy looked up, clearly surprised at his tone. "Snuggling," she answered and dropped a kiss on the head of the dog pressed against her side.

"Cocoa's not friendly," he said. "She bites."

"This dog?" Lucy asked, glancing between the brindled shepherd–pit bull mix and Caden. "Are you sure?"

"She was abused by her owner," he explained, "and she's pregnant."

"Aww," Lucy murmured, running her hand down the dog's side and rubbing Cocoa's enlarged belly. "I wondered about that."

"Seriously, Lucy. I'm working with her, but she's not

safe around people yet. I think she'll calm down once the puppies are born, but..."

He trailed off as the dog tipped up her chin and delicately licked Lucy's cheek.

"You're gonna be a mama," Lucy cooed.

Caden felt his mouth drop open. Cocoa would barely let him touch her, and she'd had to be muzzled and sedated when the vet first came to examine her.

Jase Crenshaw, an attorney in town, and one of the few people Caden had befriended in high school, had called him about the dog. Jase grew up in a trailer park on the outskirts of Crimson, and while moving his dad from there a month ago, he'd found Cocoa chained to a stump in below-freezing temperatures. Part of the dog's ear was missing and she had scars on her face and neck like she'd been used as a fighter.

Jase had called Caden along with the county humane society, and after animal enforcement had threatened the owner with charges, the owner had told Caden to go ahead and shoot the dog because she was so damn mean he'd never rehabilitate her.

The man was the only one in danger of being shot, but Jase had convinced Caden the guy wasn't worth the trouble.

Instead, Caden had managed to get near enough to the dog to unchain her, then lure her into a crate. She'd growled low under her breath the entire time but snapped only when Jase got too close. It was as if she'd recognized in Caden another spirit that knew what it was like to be truly unwanted.

Even the animal control officer had labeled the dog a lost cause, but Caden hadn't been willing to give up on her. He'd wanted to lash out at the world after his mom died and he was dumped in the foster-care system.

He'd given Garrett every reason to kick him out on multiple occasions, but his adoptive father had been consistent in his love, and eventually Caden had found a fragile kind of peace in his world. It never changed who he was at his core, but it made life more manageable.

He'd planned on taking as much time as needed to gain Cocoa's trust, but Lucy had accomplished the impossible in a matter of minutes.

What was it about her that made the nearly feral dog trust her so quickly?

He laughed under his breath. Hell, wasn't he just the same? As much as he knew she wasn't good for him, he'd been putty in her hands from the start.

"Please come out of her pen."

The dog turned her head as he spoke and gave him a baleful look.

"Don't worry," Lucy said gently as she straightened. "I'll come back and visit with you tomorrow."

Caden held his breath as Cocoa stood and pushed her big block head into Lucy's leg. He half expected the dog to become aggressive. His muscles remained tense, ready to intervene if things went south, as Lucy walked forward.

Cocoa let out a high-pitched whine, then walked to the corner of the pen, turned around twice and settled on the bed of fresh hay he'd given her earlier that morning.

He grabbed Lucy's arm and pulled her close as soon as she shut the door to the stall. "You scared the hell out of me."

She tipped up her head to look at him. "Caden, she's a sweetheart."

"I've never seen anything like that. Are you sure you don't have experience as an animal trainer?"

Lucy grinned. "I had a goldfish I won at a carnival in third grade. But he died after a week."

He laced his fingers with hers and headed toward the back of the barn. "How do you know it was a boy?"

"Because I named him Fernando," she said matter-of-factly.

"Of course you did. Want to help me feed the cats?"

"As long as none of them try to escape."

He reached up onto a high shelf and pulled down a plastic crate. "Not when it's dinnertime."

They walked into the room to a chorus of plaintive meows. He handed Lucy the container of food and pointed to the bowls. "You can put a scoop in each. They'll love you forever."

"I like the sound of that," she said, and his heart squeezed in a way that had him pressing his fingers to his chest.

She laughed as the cats and kittens tumbled around her. Caden was secretly relieved she seemed to enjoy his crazy menagerie of pets. He'd always had a thing for stray animals but sometimes felt embarrassed sharing that part of himself with other people.

It wasn't until Erin MacDonald had heard about the animals he used as therapy pets and asked him to bring them to visit her after-school program for at-risk kids that he went more public with his adoption efforts. Before that, it had mainly just been word of mouth leading him to match animals with good families.

"I'm glad you're helping with the adoption event," he told Lucy now.

She'd picked up one of the kittens and was snuggling it under her chin. "Really?"

She seemed as surprised by his words as he was saying them. "Yeah. I have a sense for where an animal belongs, but marketing isn't my thing."

"I never would have guessed." She placed the tiny cat back with his brothers and sisters and took a step away from the animals. "I wasn't sure you'd agree to my involvement, but I've already been working on some ideas. I have a Facebook page started for the event, and I'd like to take some pictures of the animals tomorrow for publicity. I read online that good photos are one of the things that can attract people to rescue animals. Erin and I have been texting. We're going to talk to local businesses about donating items for baskets to raffle. Katie Crawford at the bakery has agreed to provide cookies during the event."

"Is that all?" Caden asked with a stunned laugh.

Lucy frowned. "You're joking?"

He moved closer, smoothed her dark hair away from her face and placed a kiss on her forehead. "I'm joking. Thank you for taking care of all of that, especially after I was such an ass."

"I'm getting used to it," she said, poking him in the chest. "Lucky for you, your skills in the kitchen make up for your surly personality."

"It's time to say good-night to the animals," he said, laughing. It felt odd to have a woman teasing him. Oddly wonderful.

Lucy made a point of petting each of the dozen cats in the room before leaving. Caden checked the barn's heater, then turned down the lights, and they walked in silence back to the house. Stars lit the night sky, and the waning moon reflected softly against the snow.

At one point, Lucy slipped on a patch of ice and he put a hand around her waist to steady her. The innocent touch made his body yearn for more. He wanted her out of her layers of clothes and in his bed.

Without the distraction of dinner or the animals, the desire that had pounded through him earlier came back in full force. He wanted Lucy in a million different ways, any way she would have him. But he had to stay strong and keep his need for her under control.

Tonight had been amazing and he didn't want to ruin the tenuous friendship they'd established by taking advantage of her.

So when he opened the door to the house and followed her in, he had every intention of retreating up the stairs and locking himself in his bedroom if that's what it took.

But as soon as the door shut behind him, Lucy turned and lifted up on tiptoe, pressing her mouth to his like she'd been waiting to do it all night.

How could he resist that sort of invitation?

For a moment, Lucy wasn't sure how Caden was going to react to her kiss. He went perfectly still, his mouth not moving against hers. Maybe she'd misread the connection between them.

Maybe it was one-sided.

Then he wrapped his arms around her and lifted her off her feet. His lips parted and his tongue met hers, pulling a low groan from her throat.

She held on as he moved forward, depositing her gently onto the couch. She tugged off her hat and gloves, then unzipped her heavy coat. Her mouth went dry as he shrugged out of his jacket, leaving him standing in front of her in just the white T-shirt and jeans.

Suddenly nothing in the world was more important than touching his body. She lifted to her knees and pulled the hem of his shirt up and over his head.

"Wow," she whispered as she took in his muscled body. His shoulders looked even broader now, and there was a faint sprinkling of hair across the planes of his chest. She could clearly see the tattoo on his biceps, an eagle holding a tattered American flag.

"Good wow?" he asked. "Or 'wow, you're weird looking'?"

She bit down on her lower lip as she stared into his green eyes. "Good wow."

"Right back at you."

She laughed. "I haven't done anything to wow you yet."

"You don't have to," he murmured. "You wow me every second without even trying."

Heat pooled low in her belly and, emboldened by his words, she lifted her palms to his bare skin. She ran them through the patch of hair on his chest, noticing that he sucked in a breath as she grazed his nipples.

He pulled her closer, kissing her like a man who'd been thinking about doing just that for a very long time. The kiss was an exploration, deep and soulful, and she lost herself in the sensation of it. His hands skimmed under her shirt, making goose bumps rise on her skin as his calloused fingers trailed up her spine. Then he moved them around to her front, skimming his thumbs across her nipples and making desire spike through her.

She wanted him so badly, but something inside her head warned her she was moving too fast.

Then a different voice told her to go for it. It felt like an ice-cold glass of water splashed in her face because that second voice sounded like her mother telling her this was exactly where she wanted Caden—wrapped around her finger.

She wrenched away, scrambling to the far side of the couch like she was a teenager caught making out with her boyfriend after prom.

Caden stared at her, his green eyes cloudy with lust.

"We can't," she whispered miserably.

He blinked and seemed to come back to himself, grabbing his shirt from the floor and putting it on again. Lucy wanted to cry out in protest, but she only straightened her clothes and stood up to face him.

"It's not that I don't want to—"

"I get it."

"You don't." How could he when she barely understood it herself? She couldn't be with him because somehow her mother would find a way to use their relationship to her own ends. Lucy couldn't do that to Caden.

Or herself.

"Thank you for a lovely evening," she said, feeling like a fool for sounding so formal. "I'll get to work on plans for the adoption event first thing tomorrow morning."

Better to keep things businesslike between them. As if that was even a possibility given how her heart ached watching the warmth and desire disappear from his eyes.

"Sure," he agreed, and she rushed past him and up the stairs to her bedroom. She moved to the connecting bathroom and washed her face, then brushed her teeth and put on her pajamas like this was a normal night.

Like her stomach wasn't pitching and swirling with regret and unfulfilled need.

She climbed into bed a few minutes later and heard the creak of floorboards as Caden made his way upstairs. Longing filled her as she imagined him in his bed. Did she dare to even consider what he wore to bed? No way.

She was glad he hadn't decided to spend another night in the barn but wondered how she'd ever fall asleep knowing he was across the hall.

Chapter Eight

Lucy stumbled down the stairs and made a beeline for the coffeepot in the kitchen, as had become her habit at the ranch. Back in Florida, she didn't allow herself to drink a cup of coffee until ten o'clock, a little ritual she had to monitor her caffeine intake.

But sleep remained elusive in Colorado, and she had no doubt it was because she went on high alert every time Caden was nearby. Annoyingly, even when they weren't in the same room. She could tell where he was in the house just by the humming low in her belly and the prickling of her skin. Her mind remained committed to keeping her distance, but her body definitely hadn't gotten the memo.

She hadn't seen much of him since the night she'd run out of the living room like a big scaredy-cat, afraid of the things he made her feel and the cost for both of them if she acted on those feelings.

As if she had a sixth sense, Maureen called to check on whether Lucy had made any progress on convincing Caden that the marriage was a good idea. Much to her mother's irritation, Lucy hemmed and hawed when giving an answer.

"You should borrow one of my push-up bras," Maureen told her. "That would help attract his attention."

Lucy's face flamed hot, both at the thought that her mother was not so subtly pimping her out and at the memory of Caden's hands on her breasts. She was certain she didn't need a push-up bra for him to notice her.

"That's rude," she whispered to her mother, but Maureen only snorted.

"You have a lot to learn, Lucy-Goose. Garrett and I are having the most wonderful time." Her voice turned forlorn. "But I hate to have to worry about things back in Colorado."

"You wouldn't have to worry if he knew the full truth," Lucy countered.

"Room service is at the door," Maureen said instead of answering the accusation. "I'll call you in a few days."

Lucy tossed the phone to the counter, grabbed a mug from the cabinet and filled it to the brim with steaming coffee.

She was used to eating breakfast alone, with Caden out the door each morning long before sunrise. She'd gone on Pinterest the day after their meal together and filled a board with easy dinner recipes, then headed to the grocery store in Crimson with a mile-long list, resolved to finally learn to cook.

If her hot rancher could whip up a decent meal, surely she could put together some ingredients. And she was determined to spend time in the kitchen without any weird emotional trauma left over from her childhood.

She'd started with spaghetti sauce, which hadn't turned out half-bad. In fact, Caden had said it was the best he'd ever had, but she was pretty sure he was lying. Not that she didn't appreciate the compliment.

That was the routine they'd fallen into for the past couple of days. He was off to work on the ranch before sunrise, generously making a fresh pot of coffee and timing it to brew at seven, which was exactly when she came downstairs. She didn't bother to ask how he knew her sleep schedule.

She worked on the adoption event in the mornings, then had lunch with Caden and Chad, who came in from whatever they were doing like clockwork every day at noon.

Chad continued to flirt, which never failed to amuse Lucy, but it was the discreet ways Caden found of nudging her or pressing a palm to the small of her back as he passed that kept her senses reeling.

She'd been embarrassed that first afternoon to invite him to have dinner with her, but he'd grinned and nodded, telling her she was the best way of motivating him to get his work done.

He hadn't kissed her again, but she knew he wanted to—and thoughts of his mouth on her body filled her mind at the most inconvenient times. Like this morning when she'd been making a pitch to the local feed-and-supply store to offer discounts on pet supplies to anyone who adopted at tomorrow's event.

After showering and changing into jeans and a sweatshirt, she grabbed the deep purple down jacket she'd bought in town. Although the wind blowing against her face as she crossed to the barn was brisk, the bright sun made the morning feel not as frigid. Or maybe she was getting used to the cold, or beginning to appreciate the concept of "dry" cold, as the women at the bakery referred to Colorado's climate.

She let herself into the barn and headed for Cocoa's pen, greeting many of the other animals along the way. The dog trotted over to the door, and Lucy let her out for a short walk up the driveway. Cocoa didn't like to interact with the other dogs, so Lucy tried to give her extra attention each day. It seemed like her belly was getting rounder each time Lucy visited the barn, and Caden had told her that the puppies were due the following week.

Lucy had never been around newborns of any kind and couldn't wait for the tiny pups to make their arrival into the world.

Cocoa sniffed at the snow, did her business near the edge of a snowbank, then turned for the barn.

"Getting tired, Mama?" Lucy asked, and the dog gazed up at her with those big chocolate eyes that melted Lucy's heart.

She'd taken photos of Cocoa along with the other animals, although Caden had assured her he wouldn't be adopting the dog out until after the puppies were weaned and she'd had some time to adjust to regular dog life.

"Every time I see you with her it makes me wonder if you were a dog trainer in a former life."

Lucy turned from latching Cocoa's pen to find Caden at the far end of the barn.

"Highly doubtful," she told him.

"This place looks great." He gestured to the strands of lights strung down the barn's center walkway and the pink garland and trimmings she'd hung on the door of each pen.

"I recycled my mom's decorations," she said, stating the obvious.

"I don't know why, but all the pink works in the barn."

"I'm glad you like it." She stepped closer. "Are you nervous?"

He stared at her for a long moment and she saw his throat bob as he swallowed. "About what?"

"The adoption fair is tomorrow. Do you worry that your babies won't find homes?"

"They've got a home," he said, his voice a low rumble, "for as long as they need one."

Lucy had never understood the phrase "ovaries clenching" until this moment. She blinked away tears and willed her heart to stop stuttering. The craziest part was that Caden wasn't even trying to impress her with his sweetness.

She'd certainly had guys turn on the charm—men like Chad who made a game out of seduction. Lucy had fallen for her share of pretty lines when she'd been younger and desperate for someone to call her own. But she liked Caden best when he was simply being himself.

"Do you worry that they *will* find homes?" she asked when she trusted her voice enough to speak normally.

Caden lifted a brow.

"You'll have to let them go," she clarified, "and I know you love them."

He shrugged. "They don't truly belong to me, and if I know they'll be happy, that's enough."

Will you let me go so easily? she wanted to ask but was smart enough to keep her mouth shut. Even though they'd forged a tentative friendship and attraction simmered under the surface every time they were together, she didn't fool herself into thinking it was something lasting. Caden would not only let her go, he'd probably be relieved to escort her to the county line or whatever the equivalent of the ole heave-ho was here in Colorado.

"It's good to hear you say that," she lied, "because I have a feeling a lot of people are going to be bringing home new family members for Christmas this year."

"If they do, it's because of you."

She shook her head. "I only highlighted the work you've done with these animals."

He reached out and pulled her closer, dipping his head to press his mouth to hers. Her body tingled as she breathed him in and wound her arms around his neck. She loved that she could feel his heart beating wildly in his chest.

"It's you," he whispered, his breath tickling her skin. "All of it is you."

She knew it was the two of them together. How could she not believe in the magic of Christmas when everything she'd ever wished for seemed to be coming true?

Lucy had never been one for delayed gratification, but her years of loneliness and disappointment almost felt worth it if they'd led her to Caden.

"I have to run into town," she said, breaking the embrace before she did something stupid like whip off all her clothes in the middle of the barn. "I'm picking up coupons for a free initial vet visit from Dr. Johnson's office."

"Megan donated vet visits?" Caden rubbed a hand over his jaw, the sound of it making Lucy want to moan.

Who knew stubble was such a turn-on? "I'll remember to thank her."

Lucy crossed her arms over her chest, thinking of the petite blonde veterinarian she'd met yesterday and how the woman had been so effusive in her praise of Caden's work with unwanted animals in the area. "Thank her from a polite distance."

"Are you jealous?" Caden asked, laughing softly.

"No," she muttered. "You are free to frolic with whomever you choose." She flipped her hair over her shoulder and pretended to adjust the wreath hanging from one of the stall doors. "There's nothing between us."

"I disagree." Caden came up behind her, nuzzling his face into the side of her neck. "There's way too much between us." He nipped at her earlobe and her knees went weak. "Although I wish there was nothing."

She turned her head to glance at him as disappointment coursed through her. "You do?"

"No jackets, no shirts or jeans." He trailed kisses along the side of her neck. "Nothing but skin on skin and you in my bed."

"Oh," she breathed and sagged against him. If she'd been wondering how Caden felt about her, that pretty much summed it up. Every inch of Lucy's body felt like it was on fire and she stumbled a step when he moved away.

"You're the only woman," he told her, tapping a finger to her nose, "with whom I want to do any frolicking. Remember that, Lucy."

A moment later Chad called to him from the barn's entrance and Caden walked away.

Lucy turned back around, gripping the wooden posts

on the door of Cocoa's pen. The dog whined and gave her an almost-sympathetic look.

"I know," Lucy whispered. "Men. Canine or human, they're trouble. Every one."

Despite what he'd told Lucy, nerves skittered through Caden's stomach as the first cars pulled up the driveway and parked in front of the barn the following morning.

"It's like a caravan of adopters," Erin said next to him. Lucy had recruited Erin, David, Katie Crawford from the bakery, her husband, Noah, and a few other women she'd met in town in the past couple of days to volunteer at the event. Some of them had dogs on leashes while others were tasked with introducing the cats and bunnies to prospective families. "I can't believe she put all of this together in a week."

"It's amazing," he agreed.

Erin nudged him. "You mean *she's* amazing."

He glanced down at the grinning schoolteacher. "Yeah," he admitted, "that's what I mean." There was no use denying it. He was falling for Lucy. After their interlude in the barn yesterday, he'd seriously contemplated lifting the self-imposed ban he had on kissing her in the house.

He'd told himself that if he kept things platonic when they were together anywhere near a bed, that would keep both of them safer. But Caden didn't want to be safe with Lucy. He wanted to claim her and make her his, and he was pretty certain his heart had leaped eons ahead of his body on that count.

She'd managed to find her way past all the walls and defenses he'd erected. He wasn't sure how long he could continue to resist the attraction that drew him to her like a magnet against steel.

Then his phone rang, his dad calling from New York City. Garrett sounded like a lovestruck schoolboy as he'd told Caden about the trip. Caden wanted his dad to be happy, but he still didn't believe that was possible with Maureen. The fallout of another blow so soon after he'd started to recover from Tyson's death could be devastating for Garrett.

As much as Caden wanted Lucy, his needs were nothing compared to protecting his father. He owed everything to Garrett. How could he put that aside because of his own desires?

"You look about as welcoming as a nest of wasps."

Lucy's voice broke into his thoughts and he realized she'd taken Erin's place next to him. "I know they're your babies," she said, "but it's time to find them good homes. Put a smile on that handsome face, cowboy, and dust off your charm. It's showtime."

He watched her walk forward and greet the families emerging from cars. She was a natural with people, but he felt the old fear about being judged a punk kid who'd only cause trouble rise to the surface. What if he scared people off or they didn't appreciate the animals he'd rescued?

His gaze snagged on a couple climbing out of a minivan at the end of the row of cars. The woman, who looked to be in her midthirties, opened the back door and took the hand of a small girl in a pair of rainbow-patterned leggings, a fur-lined puffy pink coat and long braids. The girl seemed reluctant to move forward, eyeing the barn like it was some kind of medieval torture chamber.

Something shifted in Caden's chest, and all his nerves disappeared as he remembered the old Border collie mix that had come to greet him the first time he'd visited the ranch.

The ancient ranch dog had ambled up to him, sniffed at his skinned knee, then nudged his hand with a wet nose until Caden bent to pet him. "If Otis likes you, you're in," Tyson had said, already having decided that Caden was meant to be his brother.

Having never been "in" before, Caden didn't realize what that meant, but the dog's unequivocal acceptance had actually allowed him to believe he might be worth choosing.

"Mind if I borrow this one?" he asked David, grabbing the leash of the rescue dog David was holding instead of waiting for an answer. The pale yellow Lab at the end of it walked at his side as he approached the small family.

"Welcome," he called. The girl moved behind her mother's legs and the dad gave him a tight smile.

"Great setup you've got here," the man said.

"Y'all looking to add a furry friend to your household?"

The couple exchanged a look. "I'd like a dog," the man said after a moment. "I've always had one, but my wife isn't so sure."

"I got bitten when I was a child," the woman said tightly. "Dogs aren't my thing, and Macy is afraid of them."

"Because you've taught her to be," the man said under his breath.

The woman's shoulders stiffened and the little girl gripped her leg. "I don't know why I let you talk me into this."

"Because, Jen, a kid needs a dog," the man insisted.

"Does she look like she wants a dog?" Jen shot back.

"Dogs aren't for everyone," Caden agreed easily. "But sometimes all it takes is the right animal for the right family."

He bent and gave the Lab next to him a gentle head scratch. "Sage here is a great example. She's hoping to find a good home today, but she's a special dog."

"I really don't want a big dog," the woman offered.

"I do," her husband shot back.

"Why is she special?" the girl asked, peeking around her mother's legs.

"Well, now," Caden said conversationally, "she wasn't exactly taken care of properly at her last home. Sage likes to get in water, but her owner didn't dry out her ears and she got a real bad infection in them. She can't hear anymore."

"That's sad," the woman murmured, her attention on the Lab.

Caden lowered himself to kneel next to the dog. "She doesn't mind much, but she'll need a fenced-in yard and to be on a leash when she's outside so she doesn't get lost."

"We've got a fenced-in yard," Macy offered.

"Do you, now?" Caden rubbed the dog's side and Sage immediately flopped onto her back to expose her belly. "Sage also likes to be petted. Some dogs have a lot of energy, but not her. She's only three, but sometimes I call her the breathing footstool. She likes a slow walk around the block or a short hike, but mainly she wants to be loved."

"I love her," the little girl whispered and crouched down to pet the dog.

"Macy," her mother said in an exasperated tone, "this is the first dog you've seen. I haven't even agreed to adopting one."

As if sensing the trio needed to be won over, Sage rolled to her feet. She licked the little girl's face, then moved to the woman, plopping down on her butt and gazing up with a look of pure canine adoration.

"She likes you," the husband said.

Jen looked unconvinced but tentatively lowered a hand to give the dog an awkward head pat.

"She's been certified as a therapy dog," Caden told them. "Her temperament is perfect for kids."

Sage lowered her front paws and basically draped herself across the woman's feet. "She's pretty sweet," Jen murmured.

"Can we adopt her, Mommy?" Macy asked.

Jen shared a look with her husband. "I don't know…" She broke off as the dog let out a loud fart.

"She smells like Daddy," Macy shouted, earning a laugh from her mother and an eye roll from her dad.

"Of course," Caden said, "there are other dogs available. And we have cats and bunnies if a dog isn't right for your family."

"What do you think, honey?" the man asked.

The woman shrugged. "She smells like you. If that isn't a sign…"

Macy gave a loud whoop of delight. Jen stared at Caden. "I can't believe we've been here less than five minutes and now I'm adopting a dog. I don't know anything about dogs."

"I know plenty," her husband assured her.

The woman's eyes widened. "What happens when you're at work?" she asked her husband.

"She's well behaved, but I can recommend a great dog trainer if you want some extra help with her," Caden said, handing the leash to Macy. "It's important that you all feel comfortable handling her. Especially because she's deaf."

"I'd like that," Jen said, nodding.

"Sage is a very lucky dog," Lucy said from behind Caden. "If you all would just head inside, our volunteers can help you get checked out and start you off with a bag of supplies and Sage's records."

The husband clapped Caden on the shoulder as he walked by. "Thanks, man. I never thought she'd agree to this."

"Give me a call if there are any issues or you need help during the transition. We'll make sure everything goes smoothly."

The man gestured to his wife and daughter. "It already has."

Caden had been so focused on Sage meeting the small family, he hadn't realized the driveway was quickly filling with more cars.

"You did it," he said, pulling Lucy in for a hug and dropping a kiss on the top of her head.

She grinned up at him. "I watched that whole exchange. How did you know Sage was the right dog for that family?"

"The woman looked terrified and her husband was like a kid on Christmas morning. I could tell he'd want a bigger dog, and Sage is about as gentle as they come. She's perfect for a mom without much experience, but Labs still have the 'cool' factor to make the man happy."

"You have a pretty awesome 'cool' factor going on yourself," she said but ducked away when he would have lowered his mouth to hers. "We're on the job, cowboy. Back to work. You've got a barn full of animals to match."

The rest of the day flew by in a blur. Caden knew that a big part of the reason the event was so successful was Lucy's marketing efforts. Her photos of the animals were intimate and personal, the total opposite of normal shelter mug shots. She'd made individual identification cards for each animal, highlighting what made them special.

She'd been at the ranch only a week but had managed to capture the spirit of what he wanted to accomplish through rescuing the unwanted pets and finding them new homes.

Of course, Caden was also scared as hell that she'd captured his heart, something he hadn't thought possible for himself.

But every moment he spent with her was a revelation, tiny scraps of his defenses peeling away with each smile she gave him.

By the end of the day, the only animals left were the ones that belonged to him—a couple of barn cats, Cocoa and Fritzi, the therapy rabbit, plus her bonded mate, Julius. In fact, he had a waiting list of prospective adopters looking for animals. He'd referred several families to the local humane society, but a few insisted that he be the one to match them with the right rescue animal.

It was a daunting task, but Caden had been getting calls about unwanted animals that needed to be rehabilitated and rehomed on almost a weekly basis. He didn't have room for all of them, but if he could develop a pipeline of families waiting to adopt, that would certainly help him continue to save more animals.

As the last of the volunteers left at the end of the day, he got ready to do his evening chores. He said his goodbyes, weirdly touched at how invested the people of Crimson were in his little rescue operation. He knew this community was special, although he'd kept himself at arm's length from most people after the fiasco of falling for his brother's girlfriend.

"If you feel like coming into town later," David told him, shaking his hand, "we'll be at Elevation. There's a cold beer and a huge plate of wings with your name on them."

"Thanks," Caden said, then stopped himself from refusing the invitation outright. It might be nice to take Lucy out on a real date, and hanging out with friends was as good a place as any to start. "Maybe we'll see you later."

Erin smiled. "I knew you liked her," she said quietly.

He rolled his eyes. "I'll admit it. You were right. Does that make you happy?"

"Ecstatic," she said with a laugh.

"You'll never hear the end of it," David warned him, then took Erin's hand. "Better bring earplugs to town tonight."

The truth was, Caden didn't even mind giving Erin credit for realizing what he'd been too stubborn to admit from the moment he met Lucy. She was amazing.

He glanced around and saw her in deep conversation with Katie Crawford. He left the barn and headed toward the pasture that bordered the forest to check on the herd. The sooner he finished, the sooner he could get back to Lucy.

The sun sank behind the snowcapped peak of Crimson Mountain as he drove his truck across the property.

The cattle were lowing as he approached the field where they grazed on the hay Chad had put out for them. He climbed out of the truck and scratched one of the big cows between her ears, his chest tightening at the thought of the empty barn.

Lucy had been right when she'd said he loved each of the animals he rescued, even though he knew he was only a stop on their journey to a happily-ever-after.

But when the last cat had been boxed up in a carrier and put into the car with its new owner, Caden realized his life would be a little emptier until a new crop of animals came into his care.

He'd just turned back for the barn when Lucy came running across the field, her arms waving frantically.

He headed toward her, his heart stammering when she tripped and went down on all fours in the snow. The snow was packed down in some places but not others, and she could easily posthole through and twist an ankle.

"Stop," he called when she'd gotten up and begun running again.

"It's Cocoa," she shouted in response. She was close enough to him now that he could see the panic in her dark eyes. "Something's wrong. You have to help her."

He reached her, cupping her cold, tearstained cheeks in his gloved hands.

"Something's wrong, Caden. I think the babies are coming and she can't handle it. She has to be okay. The babies have to be okay."

"Shh, honey," Caden soothed as he took her hand and headed for the house. "I'll make sure she's fine." It was a promise he prayed he'd be able to keep.

Chapter Nine

"Grab towels from the closet in the hallway upstairs, plus scissors from the first-aid kit, rubbing alcohol and dental floss in case I need to tie off any of the umbilical cords." Caden didn't turn around as he issued the order, all of his attention focused on the pregnant dog.

They'd moved Cocoa into the laundry room of the main house the night before, when Caden had finished the whelping box he'd built for her.

Although Caden assured her it was a normal part of the process, it had broken Lucy's heart that the animal didn't seem to know how to settle on the bed of blankets Lucy had given her. It was as if Cocoa didn't trust something so soft. Instead, she'd curled up next to the makeshift bed on the hardwood floor, letting out a heavy sigh.

When Lucy had come in the house after the volunteers went home, Cocoa finally climbed into the whelping box, pawing at the blankets and tearing apart the sheets of newspaper as if she was making a true nest.

Lucy had let the dog out back for a potty break, then scooped a bowl of kibble and put it on the floor next to the bed. She'd gone upstairs for a shower, but when she'd returned to check on Cocoa, she realized something wasn't right.

The dog was lying on her side on top of the newspaper, her chest rising and falling in shallow pants like she was having trouble getting air. She moaned softly when Lucy touched her but hadn't moved despite Lucy's gentle coaxing.

Then Lucy had noticed a black, tarry discharge on the blankets, and she'd thrown on boots and rushed out to find Caden.

Worry making her movements jerky, she gathered the supplies and returned to the laundry room.

"She's in labor," Caden said, running a gentle hand over Cocoa's belly.

"And it's all going like it should?" Lucy asked, dropping to her knees next to him just outside the whelping box.

"Maybe," he answered, but she could tell from his tone that there were complications.

"What is it?"

He shook his head. "It seems like the first pup should have come out by now. You can see the contractions rolling across her belly, and she's pushing, but this dark-green-and-black discharge isn't normal."

"So what do we do now?"

"We wait."

"Shouldn't we call Dr. Johnson or—"

"Megan's office is an hour's drive from the ranch, and she lives another twenty toward Aspen. That's when the roads are dry. By the time she gets out here, we won't need her. We have to believe Cocoa can do this on her own."

Lucy wasn't a big fan of having faith in anything, but now she smoothed a hand over the dog's head and whispered, "You've got this, girl. We believe in you. You're so tough, and these puppies can't wait to meet their mama."

It wasn't until Caden pulled her against his side that she realized tears were dripping down her face as she spoke. She turned her head in to his shoulder and cried. He didn't try to give her false hope or tell her to pull it together. But the way he held her was far more comforting that she ever could have imagined.

"Take a look," he whispered after a minute.

Lucy sniffed and wiped at her cheeks, turning to the dog. She lifted one of her back legs as her vulva expanded and a dark sac appeared under her tail.

"It's happening," she said.

"Yeah," he agreed. "Let's give her a little space." They moved away slightly and watched as Cocoa lifted her head and began to lick at the puppy that had just been born. She gently broke the thin membrane that surrounded the pup with her teeth and chewed through the umbilical cord.

"I've never seen anything like this," Lucy whispered as the dog roughly licked at the puppy's face until it began to wriggle and cry. She nudged it with her nose and adjusted its position so that the baby could latch on and begin suckling.

The puppy continued to whimper and whine, much like any newborn crying after it came into the world. Cocoa licked the pup a few more times, as if comforting the tiny creature, then laid her head to rest on the blanket.

"Usually the puppies are born within around thirty

minutes of each other," Caden explained, "but if Cocoa needs more rest between births, it could take longer."

Lucy lost track of time as they watched the dog and her growing brood of puppies. It could have been minutes or hours or days, but she couldn't take her eyes off the miracle taking place before them.

Between each puppy's arrival, Cocoa rested, then would begin to shift and stand, pacing the small space inside the whelping box as her labor intensified. During these times, Caden and Lucy put the pups in a laundry basket lined with blankets that had a heating pad underneath so Cocoa wouldn't inadvertently hurt them.

Finally there were six tiny, wet, squirming puppies, all latched onto their mother.

"She did it," Lucy murmured, a fresh round of tears flooding her eyes.

"She's not done yet," Caden said, his voice low and serious.

Cocoa had seemed almost relaxed as the first six puppies had been born, but now she moaned and strained as if she was in distress.

Lucy sucked in a breath. "She's in pain. Are there more? You have to do something."

A muscle ticked in Caden's jaw as he shifted forward to gently massage the dog's distended belly. He whispered soothing words to her and Lucy wondered whether she or Cocoa took more comfort in his strong, steady presence.

Finally another sac emerged partway from the birth canal, and it was clear the last pup was coming out feet-first. Cocoa didn't seem to have the strength to push it out, so Caden carefully pulled the pup from her body.

This one was the smallest of the litter and the only one that didn't move.

"What's wrong?" Lucy asked even though she already feared the answer she'd receive.

Cocoa gave the puppy a few licks, then turned her attention back to the others crowding around her belly. Caden ripped the membrane away from the pup's nose and mouth and used a towel to vigorously rub its body. After a minute, his movements stopped.

"Stillborn," he whispered, gently lifting the pup into his hands.

Lucy felt a sob rise up in her throat as she reached out a finger to touch the unmoving animal. "Not after all that."

Caden wrapped the pup in a towel and set it to the side. "Its eyes and ears aren't developed, so I'd guess the puppy has been dead for a while. She's got six to take care of now," he said quietly. "If she can…"

Cocoa had closed her eyes and her breaths were once again coming in shallow pants.

"But they're all out." Lucy could hear the panic in her own voice. "She's done."

"Give her some time," Caden urged. "Her body went through a lot."

"What if she doesn't have time?" Lucy demanded, squeezing her hands into tight fists. "The puppies need their mama. Can't we do something to help her?"

Caden wrapped his big hand around both of hers. "She's going into the third stage of labor. Her uterus will contract and she'll expel any remaining placenta, blood and fluid."

The puppies continued to nurse. "They're eating," Lucy whispered. "That's a good sign, right?"

"They're getting colostrum now." Caden's voice was calm but she could hear the worry threading through it. "Her milk should come in within a day or two."

"And if it doesn't?"

He took her hand and squeezed her fingers. "We'll take care of them."

Lucy swallowed around the lump of emotion in her throat. They'd already lost one puppy. She couldn't stand to think of the others not surviving. Even more, she needed Cocoa to be okay. There was something about the wayward dog's instinct for survival and the fact that she'd bonded with Lucy that made Lucy feel as if Cocoa belonged to her. She hadn't realized how badly she wanted something of her own until she was close to losing it.

Minutes passed, but finally Cocoa raised her head. Her body released a spurt of fluid and she shifted and turned, her pink tongue flicking out to lick the little pups once again.

"She's got it," Caden whispered.

"Keep going, Mama," Lucy told the dog in her gentlest tone. Cocoa blinked and her big chocolate gaze caught on Lucy's for a moment.

"You're doing great." Lucy spoke as though the dog could understand her, which was silly. Cocoa nudged the pups with her nose. The sounds of slurping and whimpering followed as the dogs piled on top of each other at her stomach, and Lucy finally breathed a sigh of relief.

"She needs space now." Caden picked up the towel with the stillborn puppy and stood.

"We have to bury this one." Lucy eyed the tiny bundle.

"That's going to be a challenge with the ground frozen." He met Lucy's gaze and nodded. "We'll figure it out tomorrow. I promise."

Lucy was quickly discovering that she liked being able to have faith in someone. She had no doubt that Caden's word was good.

"Thank you for being so calm during all of that. I'm sure you're used to stuff being born."

"Stuff," he repeated with a smile, setting the towel on the counter next to the washing machine.

"Animals," she clarified with an eye roll. "Baby cows and horses."

"Calves and foals," he corrected as they washed their hands.

"I know that," she said, pressing her fingers to her chest. "I can't think right now. I just..." To her embarrassment, a tremor snaked through her body and tears stung the back of her eyes. She turned away as her shoulders started to shake.

"It's okay, sweetheart," Caden murmured and pulled her close. She buried her face in his shirt, trying to regain control of herself. But with the adrenaline that had been buzzing through her now wearing off, all of her fear over Cocoa and her puppies set off an avalanche of emotions.

Caden scooped her into his arms and carried her through the house and up the stairs. She concentrated on pulling in air, trying desperately to make her heart beat a normal rhythm.

But when she opened her eyes, her heart stuttered for a different reason entirely. "This is your bedroom."

He pulled down the covers and set her on his big bed, one side of his mouth quirking. "I don't think you should be alone right now. This doesn't mean I'm expecting—"

"I don't want to be alone," she interrupted, and to hell with both of their expectations. But when she reached for him, he backed away a step.

"Give me five minutes," he instructed, lifting his hands, palms out. "Between the adoption event, the cattle and a litter of puppies, I stink like a barn. I need a shower and then—" he paused, his eyes going dark "—I'll be back."

She bit down on her bottom lip as he walked away, tugging his shirt over his head as he moved. A minute later she heard the water in the hall bathroom turn on, and her stomach dipped and whirled as it had every day for the past week as she listened to him shower and imagined…

Lucy had a vivid imagination.

She needed a shower as much as he did, but she kicked off her shoes then brought her knees to her chest and waited. For all of about thirty seconds. Then she got up and walked toward the bathroom, steam pouring out into the hallway as she let herself in. She could barely make out Caden's silhouette behind the frosted glass of the walk-in shower but stepped forward, anyway.

The shower door opened slightly and Caden's face appeared, droplets of water clinging to his skin. "You don't take direction well, do you?" he asked, his voice rumbly but laced with humor.

She shook her head. "I *really* don't want to be alone right now." She continued moving toward him, pushing open the door and walking into the shower. Her eyes drifted shut as the heat and scent of his shampoo surrounded her. "Don't mind me," she whispered. "You won't even know I'm here."

He gave a low chuckle and smoothed her wet hair away from her face. "Did you think about getting undressed first?"

"I'm done thinking for the day," she answered, earning another soft laugh.

"Works for me," he said, and she felt his fingers begin to undo the buttons of her soaking wet blouse. She dropped her head and watched his hands, big against the tiny buttons. The shirt clung to her body and she sucked in a breath when he peeled it off her shoulders.

He bent and unfastened her jeans, pushing them down over her hips and lower on her legs. She stepped out of them and felt a rush of cool air as he deposited both garments on the bathroom floor. He slid his palms up her calves, his calloused fingertips tickling the backs of her knees.

She felt him press an openmouthed kiss to her inner thigh. Heat shot through her body at the intimate caress. He straightened and cupped her cheeks in his hands.

"Look at me, Lucy," he commanded, and she opened her eyes. "This doesn't have to go anywhere right now."

"You're naked," she told him.

"I'm aware." He kissed the tip of her nose. "But you've had a hell of a day. I get that you don't want to be alone, but I also understand that doesn't mean—"

"It does mean something," she argued and leaned in to lick the base of his throat.

His groan heated all the cold places inside her as much as the hot water. He wrapped his arms around her and undid her bra with one deft movement. She let the straps fall down her arms and the bra to drop the floor, then hooked her thumbs in the waistband of her panties and pushed them over her hips.

"That's better," she whispered with a saucy smile.

"Much," he agreed and lifted his hands to cup her breasts. She whimpered when his thumbs grazed over her nipples. He bent his head to cover one tight peak, and she might have melted to a puddle on the shower floor if he hadn't been holding an arm around her waist.

As his attention switched to the other breast, Lucy threaded her fingers through his wet hair. Then he moved lower, kneeling in front of her, and sparks lit up her body like she was a firework on the Fourth of July.

Her back pressed to the cool tile as his mouth worked its magic. And when pleasure exploded through her, she cried out his name. She felt her knees start to give way again as the last bits of pleasure pulsed through her.

"Stay with me," Caden said, flattening his open hand on her belly as if to hold her up while he turned off the water.

Oh, she was with him. Too far gone to let go now.

He stepped out of the shower, grabbed a towel and wrapped it around her, not bothering to cover himself, much to Lucy's delight. His body was perfection from head to toe and everywhere in between. He scooped her into his arms, edging around the doorway so she didn't bump her head.

She scraped her fingers gently along his chest, then touched one flat nipple with the tip of her tongue. He sucked in a breath and stumbled a step.

"I'm going to end up taking you in the hall if you do that," he said, his voice hoarse.

"We should start with the bed," she answered, and a moment later they were in his bedroom again. He set her on her feet, the backs of her legs bumping the mattress.

"You're so damn beautiful," he whispered, and she knew the words should have thrilled her. What woman didn't want to receive a compliment from a handsome man who'd just given her the greatest orgasm of her life?

But a part of Lucy wanted to believe Caden saw her for more than just what she looked like. Her beauty was genetic, inherited from a mother who'd wielded her looks like a weapon. Even though Lucy knew she wasn't cut from that same cloth, she hated being judged on her looks alone.

As if reading her mind, Caden pressed a hand to her chest where her heart beat against his palm. "In here," he whispered. "Your spirit is beautiful, Lucy. You have a huge heart, and you're smart and talented. There's so much more to you than you even know."

Do you really think so?

She wanted to ask the question out loud, but that would make her needy and pathetic. And right now she didn't feel either of those things. She felt strong and cherished and truly seen by this man.

It was everything.

She laced her fingers with his and moved onto the bed, Caden following until his body covered hers. He kissed her until she was practically senseless, her body humming with need. "I want you," she whispered. "Now."

He reached to the nightstand, pulled out a condom packet, and tugged it open with his teeth.

"Let me," she told him, and rolled the condom down his length. He entered her in one thrust, and Lucy had never felt so complete as she did with Caden filling her.

"So good," he whispered. "You feel so good."

"It's not me," she answered, meeting his gaze. "It's us."

His eyes went dark at her words, and when he kissed her it was like a promise between them. They moved together as if they'd known each other for ages. Brilliant pressure built in her body as Caden both took her out of herself and kept her tethered to reality with the sweet words he whispered against her skin.

It wasn't long before Lucy broke apart again, an explosion of light and color surging through her body. A moment later she felt Caden tremble, and he let out a low groan and dropped his head into the crook of her neck.

He lifted his head a moment later and gave her a goofy half smile. "I like everything about you, Lucy. Especially having you come apart in my arms."

"I like you, too," she whispered and pretended her mind didn't want to substitute a different *l* word entirely to describe her feelings for this man. She'd settle for *like*. After all, settling was something she did quite well.

Caden watched the light turn from gray to pink as he held Lucy in his arms. Her breathing was slow and rhythmic, her body warm and pliant tucked into his.

He'd always been an early riser, convenient when living on a ranch, but this morning he wished he could stay in bed all day. He figured maybe then he could gain some kind of control around this woman. Or not, if last night was any indication.

After that first time, they'd dressed and gone back downstairs to check on Cocoa and her puppies. The dog and the six little pups already seemed bigger. Caden had attached a different-colored piece of rickrack around each of their necks to tell them apart, and it was funny to already see distinct personalities emerging.

He knew it still bothered Lucy that Cocoa had lost one of the puppies, but Caden realized how lucky they were that the others were healthy. He and Lucy had shared a simple meal of sandwiches and salads as they watched the animals. He'd worried that the intimacy that had rocked his world might have comprised their tentative friendship, but instead he felt even more connected to Lucy.

When Cocoa and the pups were settled again, Lucy had taken his hand and led him back upstairs. They'd undressed each other slowly, hands and mouths exploring. He wanted to know every part of her, and for the first time he was willing to share pieces of himself he'd kept hidden.

Even when she'd run a hand over the tiny scars below his shoulder blade, he hadn't tensed.

"They look like…" she'd whispered, her voice trailing off. He understood from her tone that she'd realized exactly what had made the marks.

"Cigarette burns." He'd supplied the words she couldn't seem to form. It was the first time he'd named the scars to anyone other than Tyson. "Such a cliché, but my foster dad had a thing for that movie *The Breakfast Club*. There's a scene where one of the kids in detention talks about his father putting out a cigar on his body as punishment for a spilled can of paint. It was twisted, but he wanted to recreate—"

"Stop." Lucy had placed her hands over his back like she could erase the truth of what had happened to Caden after his mom died and he got sucked into the foster-care system.

"Don't be sad for me." He'd flipped her onto her back and wiped away the tears that slipped from the corners of her eyes. "Tyson lost his mind when he first saw the scars. I think he went home to Garrett that night and made the case for me coming to live on Sharpe Ranch."

He smiled, trying to take the edge off the horror of what he'd shared with her. Lucy's mom might be a gold digger, but from what he could tell she hadn't exposed her daughter to anything like what he'd experienced.

Lucy thought she understood him, but she had no idea how broken Caden was on the inside. "In some ways that bastard did me a favor. It got me out of there and gave me Garrett and Tyson."

Her mouth pressed into a thin line. "It never should have come to that. You were a kid."

"Bad things happen," he said simply, the only truth that had remained indisputable for his entire life.

"Good things can happen, too," she countered. "You deserve the good things, Caden."

He sucked in a breath as his heart leapt. The feeling was a strange mix of hope and caution because he'd found happiness to be all too fleeting. Besides, he wasn't sure he agreed with that statement, but he didn't bother to argue. Not when Lucy was staring at him like she could see all the way into his soul.

He dropped a kiss on her shoulder now, but she didn't stir. Her breathing changed to a soft snore that made him smile. It was difficult to believe how badly he'd misjudged her. Lucy was a light in the darkness of his lonely life. He could far too easily come to depend on her radiant brightness.

He climbed out of bed, grabbing his clothes and taking them downstairs to dress so he wouldn't disturb her. He couldn't help but think that if he'd gotten her personality and intentions so wrong, maybe he needed to give Maureen a chance.

Caden had thought he'd found love with Becca, until he'd realized she was only using him to hurt Tyson. Although it was too soon to put a name on what he felt for Lucy, his heart told him this was the real deal.

He couldn't remember a time when he'd felt so damn happy. Even more than the happiness—not to mention the afterglow from the best sex of his life—there was a peace inside him. It was as if all the jumbled parts of himself that had been clamoring around inside for years had finally found a home. He fit together now because Lucy was the piece he'd been missing.

Was it possible that Maureen did that for Garrett? They'd all lived in the halcyon shadow of Tyson's mother for so many years, it was difficult to believe Garrett could find happiness with another woman, especially someone like Maureen Renner.

But no one deserved happiness more than Garrett. If he had it with Lucy's mother, maybe Caden needed to have a little faith in his father's judgment.

Chapter Ten

After finishing his chores the next morning, Caden drove into Crimson. He knew Lucy would want to spend the day watching over Cocoa, so he planned to pick up breakfast, lunch and something easy to make for dinner.

To his surprise, he was greeted with hugs and a chorus of excited congratulations about the weekend's adoption event from the ladies behind the counter at Life Is Sweet.

One of the baristas took great pride in showing him photos on her phone of the cat she'd taken home on Saturday and immediately dressed in a superhero costume.

"I named him Wayne," she confided with a goofy grin. "He's the best."

"He looks good in a cape," Caden agreed, not sure what else to say.

The young woman scurried back around the counter to take an order as Katie and Noah Crawford walked out from the back of the store along with their toddler daughter, Ryan. Noah wore his olive green forest-service uniform. He'd been managing the local ranger district since he moved back to town a couple of years ago.

Katie wore a striped apron with Ask about My Sticky Buns embroidered across the front. He'd known both of them since middle school and would never have expected the soft-spoken baker to make a match with Noah, who before Katie had quite the reputation as a ladies' man. But contentment was written across both their faces and a little pang of envy shot through him at the sight of it.

"You're toast," Noah told him. "Everyone in town has seen your soft underbelly now. There's no going back to scowling, scary rancher man."

"I don't have a soft underbelly," Caden argued. "And I wasn't trying to scare anyone." That wasn't exactly true. He liked keeping people at a distance. It worked for him. At least, until Lucy had blown his defensive walls to smithereens.

Katie laughed. "You didn't have to try." The little girl perched on her hip stretched out her arms and dived toward Caden.

"Ryan," Katie cried. "Where do you think you're going?"

He scooped up the girl, with her riot of soft blond curls and a smudge of blueberry on her cheek. She poked at his Stetson. "Hat," she told him.

"My hat," he agreed and, balancing her in one arm, took the hat off his head and perched it on hers. She giggled as it covered her eyes.

"Ryan's hat," she shouted.

Noah glanced behind him to the coffee bar. "Now you're good with kids, too. Dude, you're going to be swarmed by single women."

Caden followed Noah's gaze and saw the three women behind the counter staring at him with looks

that ranged from mildly interested to positively predatory. Uh-oh.

"I'm not on the market," he said quickly, placing the
hat back on his head and handing Ryan back to Katie.

"Perhaps because you're already off the market?"
Katie asked, one brow raised.

"I don't know… I mean, I'm not…" Caden blew out a
breath. "I just want a bag of muffins," he said helplessly.

"I like Lucy," Katie said, leaning forward. "She's a
good fit for Crimson."

"I'm not sure about that," Caden said. "She's used
to living in Florida. Colorado winters might not be her
thing."

Katie shook her head. "I mean she's a good fit for
the community. For you."

He felt his mouth drop open and quickly snapped it
shut. "She's too good for me," he muttered.

Noah dropped a smacking kiss on the top of his
wife's head. "Those are the best kind," he offered.

"I'll get the muffins," Katie said with a laugh.

"You know," Noah said quietly, leaning in closer,
"guys finding a woman better than we deserve is sort
of a thing around here."

"I get that," Caden agreed, thinking of the men he
knew and the women who loved them. "But there's
not being good enough and there's being emotional na-
palm."

"Which are you?"

"Everyone knows what happened between Tyson and
me," Caden said through his teeth, hating to discuss the
rift with his brother but at the same time needing someone to understand. "I made some really stupid choices.
People got hurt. My brother died."

Noah took a step back. "You can't blame yourself for that. I was on duty out at Cherokee Ridge when the call came in from his buddies. The search-and-rescue captain told me it was a freak accident."

Caden's heart, which had been so full after last night, went cold at the reminder of the circumstances of Tyson's death. "If I'd been there—"

"Nothing would have changed," Noah interrupted. "You couldn't have saved him."

"I could have tried." Caden met Noah's blue gaze, daring the other man to argue.

Noah only inclined his head. "Guilt and I are old friends," he said quietly. "I can tell you she's not worth the trouble."

"Here you go," Katie said, approaching with a pink bag that had the bakery's logo on the front. "I threw in a chocolate croissant because that's what Lucy always orders."

"Thanks," Caden told her, reaching for his wallet.

Katie held up her hands. "No charge today. We had several new customers come in yesterday from the adoption event. Think of the muffins as a referral fee."

Caden wanted to argue. He didn't like to be indebted to anyone, but Noah was staring at him like he wasn't done with the conversation about Tyson.

Caden was done.

He leaned in and gave Katie and Ryan a quick hug. "Thanks again," he said and walked out of the bakery.

He was halfway down the street when a man called his name. He thought about ignoring the greeting. This morning had already been too much.

But he turned and held out a hand when Derek Lawson approached. "Morning, Derek. How are things?"

Derek ran a hand through his thinning hair, looking more agitated than Caden had ever seen him. "You tell me, Sharpe. I got a call from some chick I'd never met playing twenty questions about the way I keep your dad's books. What the hell is that about?"

Caden felt a muscle tick in his jaw but forced a casual shrug. He took a calming breath and glanced down the street toward the park that spread across an entire city block in the middle of town. There was an enormous Christmas tree decorated with handmade ornaments from kids at the elementary school and a big star on top.

A few feet from the tree was an ice-skating rink, several families were already twirling on the ice. Maybe he'd bring Lucy into town for an afternoon of holiday fun. He'd never been much for the town festivities. Never had a reason before now.

"The daughter of my dad's fiancée," he explained, keeping his voice steady.

"The one you think is after your dad's money?" Derek asked, his eyes narrowing.

"He's happy," Caden answered noncommittally. When Garrett first brought Maureen home, Caden had confessed his fear over her intentions to Derek. In specifically unflattering terms. Terms that would light up Lucy's temper like a powder keg if she ever knew. Although still not a fan of Maureen, he now regretted opening his big mouth.

"Lucy is staying at the ranch while Garrett and her mom are in New York City. She has a background in finance and he asked her to take a look at things just to give her something to do." The truth was, Caden had forgotten that his dad had given Lucy access to the business accounts. She'd done so much last week for the adoption event, he hadn't realized she was also reviewing the books.

"I didn't like the way she was talking to me," Derek told him, falling into step with him as they neared the truck. "Seemed like just as much trouble as her mom."

"Lucy's not—"

Derek stepped closer, lowered his voice. "Did you ever consider that this was the plan all along? I mean, what sort of financial background are we talking about?"

"I don't really know," Caden admitted.

"Exactly." Derek shot a finger in the air like Caden had just proven some kind of important point. "Could be this Lucy chick is casing the books for her mom to see how much the old man's truly got in the accounts. I wouldn't be surprised if she tried to act like things aren't right."

He crossed his thin arms over his chest. Derek had been a friend of Tyson's from high school. His family owned the hardware store in town and he'd gotten an accounting degree, then come back to run the business when his father had a stroke.

He'd offered to help with the Sharpe Ranch finances in the aftermath of Tyson's accident. "Wouldn't be surprised if she tried to throw me under the bus. That'd be convenient, right? She could make up issues with what I've been doing so that they can get their hands on the money."

If Derek had made his accusation against Lucy a week ago, Caden would have jumped all over it. But things had changed. He'd changed...because of her.

Yet a sliver of doubt snaked through his veins. He'd been a fool for a woman before with grave consequences. Could Lucy actually be orchestrating a con while he played right into her deception?

"She has no reason to—"

"Come on, man," Derek urged. "Don't let some woman lead you around by your junk. How many times has the mom been married?"

Caden swallowed. "This would be number four."

"Your dad hasn't been himself since Tyson died. We both know that. It could have been different if you'd been on the trip with him, but you weren't. Now we both need to look out for Garrett's best interests. It's what Tyson would have wanted."

Derek's careless words were like a punch to the gut. As much as Caden appreciated Noah Crawford's claim that there wasn't anything that could have been done differently to save Tyson, everyone knew it wasn't true. Derek had just proved it. Caden also knew that he had to protect his father against any more pain.

His feelings for Lucy had made him lose sight of his purpose for a moment, but he had to refocus on what was important in his life.

Unfortunately, his own happiness didn't count for crap.

"I appreciate everything you've done to help," he said, placing a hand on Derek's shoulder and squeezing. "Dad and I both do. I'll make sure Lucy doesn't overstep her bounds. You've got nothing to worry about."

"I hope not, man." Derek nodded. "I've got my hands full already with the store. I'm happy to help with the ranch's accounting. Anything for Tyson. But not if it means some stranger busting my—"

"I'll handle it," Caden told him. He tightened his grip on the bakery bag, placing it on the floor on the truck's back seat. Acid burned in his gut and a stale metallic taste filled his mouth. The thought of taking a bite of one of Katie's sweet baked goods made his stomach lurch. Had he really been a fool for…? Not love. It couldn't be love that he felt for Lucy.

He ignored the rest of the errands he'd planned and headed back to the ranch. The snow was creamy white under the gentle sun of early morning. He drummed his fingers on the steering wheel and concentrated on pulling air in and out of his lungs.

He didn't want to give any credence to the insinuations Derek made toward Lucy and her mother. He wanted to go back to last night and the sweetness of holding Lucy in his arms.

She was in the mudroom, cross-legged on the floor in a pair of black yoga pants and a stretchy top, when he walked in. She grinned up at him, a mug of coffee cradled in her hands. His heart stammered at the tenderness in her eyes. "Cocoa is such a sweet mama," she whispered, "and the puppies are already developing their own personalities." She pointed to the darkest of the pups. "This one is the leader, but the one with the purple rickrack gives him a run for his money."

"We need to move them back out to the barn," he said coolly. "Garrett doesn't allow pets in the house."

"I bet he'd make an exception for puppies," she murmured, then uncrossed her legs and stood. "I talked to my mom this morning. They got tickets to *Hamilton*, so they're going to stay in New York for an extra couple of days."

Caden bit back a curse as he pulled his phone from his jacket pocket. He'd missed a call from his dad while he was in town and there was a text message shining up at him from the home screen.

This old cowboy likes the big city. Changed flights to come home on December 22. Take care of Lucy.

"Garrett never takes vacations like this," he muttered.

"I guess it's nice they're having so much fun together," Lucy suggested quietly. "Mom sounded really happy on the phone."

"I bet she did." Caden saw Lucy's shoulders stiffen at the insinuation in his tone. "Your mom must be pretty damn good between the…" He drew in a breath, stopping the flow of ugly words before he said something he couldn't take back. "They'll return soon enough."

"What's wrong?" Lucy placed a hand on his arm, and it felt like his skin was on fire under the fabric of his work shirt.

He shrugged off her touch. "It's fine for my dad to take a break, but I've got work to do."

What he needed was to get away from Lucy and the spell she wove around him. Even now, as frustrated as he was at not being able to figure out what the hell was going on with her, he wanted to pull her close and breathe her in. To forget everything except the way she made him feel.

But he understood the price he could pay for losing himself to a woman. Nothing was worth risking that again.

"I stopped at the bakery." He thrust the pink bag into her hands. "I'll make up a place for Cocoa and her puppies in the barn when I have a break later."

Lucy frowned at him. "Caden, what's—"

He held up a hand. "I've got to get going on the day." Then he turned and walked away.

Snow flurries started coming down around lunchtime as Lucy sat in front of the computer. The house remained quiet for the next several hours as she worked on deciphering the tangled spiderweb of financial records from Garrett's various properties and business ventures.

She didn't bother making another call to the family friend who was supposedly handling the books for Sharpe Ranch. Derek Lawson had been outright rude to her when they'd spoken a few days earlier. Besides, the more she uncovered, the more certain she was that Derek was at the heart of many of the discrepancies she found.

It was good to have something to keep her busy so she wouldn't spend the whole day ruminating over Caden's bizarre behavior. Her emotions ranged from anger to shock to disappointment. Not heartbreak, of course. She couldn't have her heart in the mix after one night together, no matter how amazing that night had been.

When Erin texted and invited her to go caroling through downtown with a group of women meeting at the Crimson Community Center that night, Lucy accepted right away. She might as well put all her useless holiday song lyric knowledge to good use. Not to mention that she couldn't stand the thought of spending an awkward evening in the house with Caden either ignoring her or acting like a jerk.

She checked on the puppies, made sure Cocoa went

out for a potty break and had fresh water, then dressed and drove into town. The snow was still coming down, and she had no idea where on the property Caden and Chad were working today. She didn't bother to leave a note. Based on his behavior this morning, Caden would be happy to have an evening alone in the house.

Her little rental car slid on the snow-covered roads a couple of times, and by the time she parked around the corner from the community center, Lucy's knuckles were white from gripping the steering wheel so tightly.

The group was gathered in front of the historic brick building, and Erin waved as she approached.

"I'm so glad you could make it," Erin said, giving her a warm hug. "Let me introduce you to everyone."

Katie Crawford also hugged her. "Lucy is the publicity genius behind the success of Caden's adoption event. We're hoping she decides to stay in Crimson so I can tap her to help with the bakery's marketing plan for the summer season."

"Then I'd like to talk to her about the new campaign for the community center." A delicately beautiful woman with dark hair and pale hazel eyes stepped forward. "I can always use a fresh set of eyes. I'm Olivia Travers. Nice to meet you, Lucy."

Lucy shook Olivia's hand. "I don't really have an official background in marketing."

"But you're so good at it," Katie countered.

There were two other women in the group. Millie Travers, Olivia's sister, happened to be married to the brother of Olivia's husband. She also met Julia Crenshaw, who was the sister of Katie's husband. They were clearly a tight-knit group, and Lucy suddenly felt like the outsider she was in this town.

"Okay, Olivia," Julia said after introductions were made. "Caroling was your idea." She leaned in closer to Lucy. "My plan was to hit the Mexican restaurant for enchiladas and margaritas."

"We can do that anytime," Olivia answered. "Christmas is special and the chamber of commerce has asked certain businesses to coordinate these little caroling outings to add a bit more spirit to downtown during the holiday season."

Julia rolled her eyes. "I know. Jase told me all about it. He's very proud of what a do-gooder I've become."

Lucy tried to cover her snort, but Julia turned with a grin. "My husband heads up the chamber along with Olivia. They're the official Crimson cheerleading squad. I come along kicking and screaming."

"Or singing," Millie added, nudging her sister. "Even though Olivia can't carry a tune to save her life."

Olivia sniffed. "Jasper thinks I have a beautiful voice."

Millie laughed. "He's two," she explained to Lucy. "Can you sing?"

"Actually, yes," Lucy answered, surprised to find herself admitting the talent to these women. "I used to sing all the time when I was younger. It sounds silly now, but my mom nicknamed me Songbird." She gave a small laugh. "For a while she was convinced I could become America's next pop princess."

"No pressure," Julia said quietly.

"Exactly," Lucy agreed, recognizing sarcasm. "I didn't do well under pressure. She entered me in a few competitions at malls but it turned out that while I had the voice of an angel at home, I also suffered from horrible stage fright." She made a face. "The end of my short-lived career was the day I puked up my nervous stomach all over a panel of judges."

"Alright, then," Olivia said, linking her arm with Lucy's. "There will be no puking this evening. How about I stand in front and lip-synch and you can hide in the back and belt out the songs?"

Lucy felt warmth infuse her veins at the ease with which these women made her part of the group without judgment. No forcing her to play a part or be someone different than who she was. Being Lucy seemed to be enough for them.

They made their way to the center of downtown Crimson. Most of the shops were still open, and they stopped on the corner across from the ice-skating rink. Olivia turned to the group, pulling small booklets out of her tote bag.

Julia groaned. "We have songbooks? This is so official."

"Jase's idea," Olivia answered with a grin. "He said you have a habit of making up your own lyrics and they're not always appropriate."

Julia stuck out her tongue. "But they're fun."

"What song do we start with?" Erin asked, paging through the sheets.

"'Santa Claus Is Coming to Town,'" Millie suggested. "Everyone knows that one."

"What do you think, Lucy?" Julia asked.

"I worked retail for so many holiday seasons that I know all of them."

"Brilliant," Olivia said with a bright smile. "You're going to make us sound amazing."

"Tall order," Julia muttered, and Lucy smiled.

"Why am I suddenly so nervous?" Erin asked. "We

should have stopped at Elevation first for some liquid courage."

"Not too late," Millie offered.

Olivia narrowed her eyes at her sister. "Are we ready?"

The women nodded, each focused on her own small songbook. After a moment it was obvious no one wanted to start, so Lucy cleared her throat and began singing, "You'd better watch out..."

Erin, Millie and Julia added their voices to the mix while Olivia stepped forward and motioned to the people standing nearby to join them. By the time they got to the chorus, Lucy forgot to be nervous.

Instead she remembered how much she loved to sing. She sang the words, not even embarrassed when Julia turned and flashed a grin, her eyes wide with surprise. A few of the people on the street began singing and by the last verse, a crowd had gathered around their small group like they were buskers in some Victorian Christmas pageant.

Applause erupted as they finished and one of the men watching shouted, "'Joy to the World' next."

Olivia turned to Lucy with a questioning glance, and Lucy nodded. "You're so good," Erin whispered, squeezing her fingers.

"Thanks." Unfamiliar pride bubbled up in Lucy. It had been a long time since she'd been recognized for having talent at anything except being a pretty face. She did her best to believe in herself but sometimes it was hard to remember why she should.

She launched into a cheery rendition of "Hark! The Herald Angels Sing," then transitioned to "Rudolph the

Red-Nosed Reindeer" and led the women in "Silent Night" and "Deck the Halls."

The crowd continued to sing with them, and by the time they'd finished close to a dozen carols, Lucy realized the group had slowly pushed her to the front.

She felt her palms grow sweaty as the final song came to an end and all eyes remained on her.

Olivia threw her arms around Lucy. "That was so much fun." With Lucy hugged tight to her side, she faced the crowd. "Can we get another round of applause for the most amazing Lucy Renner?"

Lucy shook her head, but cheering and whistles from the people gathered in front of them drowned out any protest she might have offered.

"I think we have time for one more song," Olivia said, glancing at Lucy. "Is that okay with you?"

"Sure," Lucy said. The truth was she could have spent the entire evening singing.

"How about 'O Holy Night'?" a deep voice called, and Lucy's entire body went still.

She looked wildly around the faces in front of her until her gaze landed on Caden, who stood near the back of the crowd near the edge of the ice-skating rink, David and Noah flanking him.

"Good choice," Olivia called.

"It's not in the book," Erin said from behind Lucy. "I only know the 'fall on your knees' part."

"Me, too," Millie agreed.

"I'm not sure I know that much," Julia added.

Olivia frowned. "Maybe another—"

"I can do it," Lucy told her and took a step forward. "'O Holy Night' is one of my favorites. Anyone who knows it is welcome to join in."

She closed her eyes when nerves tingled down her skin, and took a deep breath to calm herself. She wasn't a scared ten-year-old girl in front of a row of jaded judges. She was helping people get into the Christmas spirit, and for once, she appreciated how magical coming together as a community during the holiday season could be.

She sang the words softly at first, feeling joy rush through her as a few people sang with her. It was one of her favorite songs, and she wondered how Caden knew to request it.

By the time she sang about hearing angel voices, Lucy could feel tears pricking the back of her eyes. Yes, she knew the words to so many holiday songs, but on this December night, surrounded by new friends and strangers, the meaning of Christmas felt real for the first time.

As the song's final note ended, a hush fell over the people gathered around their little caroling group.

"Merry Christmas, everyone," Olivia called after a moment. "Enjoy your time here in Crimson."

There was more enthusiastic clapping and then the crowd began to disperse. Millie, Julia, Erin, Katie and Olivia surrounded Lucy in one big group hug.

"Best Christmas activity ever," Millie shouted.

Julia wiped at her cheeks. "You made even a grinch like me cry, girl. Where did you learn to sing like that?"

Lucy bit down on her lip and shrugged. "I just like to sing."

Katie grinned. "The best way to spread Christmas cheer—"

"No quoting *Elf*," Julia interrupted, winding a hand around Katie's neck and clapping a hand over her mouth. "Katie and my brother love Will Ferrell. It's a problem."

"Will Ferrell is never a problem." Noah untangled his wife from Julia and kissed the top of Katie's head. "Lucy, you've got some pipes."

"Major pipes," David agreed, coming to join them. Erin pressed herself to his side. "Are you ladies in need of a thirst quencher after all that singing?"

"Absolutely," Millie told him, glancing at her phone, then to her sister. "Logan and Jake are going to meet us there. Claire is coming to the house to babysit Jasper and Brooke."

Lucy's heart fluttered as the women—her new friends—paired up with their respective men, and she tried not to look for Caden. It all seemed so easy and effortless, although she imagined each of the couples had their own story to tell.

She'd never had an expectation of getting her own happily-ever-after, so envying the people in love around her had never been an issue. But since she'd come to Crimson, so much had changed...and a lot of it had to do with her feelings for Caden.

The flutter morphed into a full-fledged racing gallop, and she didn't have to glance up to know who stood in front of her.

"How did you know that's my favorite Christmas song?" she asked, clasping her hands tight in front of her to keep from reaching for him.

They'd had one amazing night together, but that didn't mean she had any claim on him. Based on his behavior today, it didn't mean anything at all.

His mouth curved into a smile. "I didn't know, but it was the one I wanted to hear you sing. Your voice is..."

He reached out and traced a finger along her cheek. "You have the most beautiful voice I've ever heard."

"I can carry a tune," she said, loving the feel of his calloused fingertip on her skin. "It's not a big deal."

"You love to sing."

"I used to," she agreed.

"But…"

"But I don't love to perform."

"You could have fooled me. You held the entire town captive with your talent tonight."

She laughed. "I don't know about the entire town."

"Admit it. You wowed the crowd."

She tried to play it off, to stay cool and unmoved, but it was a losing battle. She felt a goofy smile split her face and did a little victory dance like a wide receiver who'd just caught a touchdown pass in the Super Bowl.

"I really did," she whispered. "Who knew all those years of listening to canned Christmas music would have prepared me for this?"

"You took my breath away," he told her, his eyes once again shining with tenderness.

"What happened this morning, Caden? I don't understand why, but it felt like we were right back where we started with you hating me."

"I never hated you."

"It certainly felt that way."

"I'm sorry," he said softly. "About how we began and how I acted this morning. Last night was amazing." He ran a hand across his jaw. "It's difficult for me to trust amazing."

"Are you two going to join us?" Erin called from across the street. "First round's on my hottie fiancé."

"We'll catch up," Lucy answered, waving the group on without them.

She studied Caden for another long moment, trying to figure out what it was he wasn't saying. "Why did you come to town tonight?"

He leaned in, brushed his mouth across hers. "For you, Lucy. I came for you."

Chapter Eleven

"You should record an album."

"Seriously, I'd pay money to hear you sing."

Caden watched as color crept into Lucy's cheeks once again. The two guys who stood in front of her were the latest in a long line of patrons at Elevation who wanted to talk to her about her voice.

She seemed flattered but uncomfortable with the attention, and his desire to take care of her intensified as she shifted closer.

"Thank you," she said with an unassuming smile and gripped the back of his shirt tighter.

He moved so he was partially blocking her from view. "Nice talking to you," he told the two guys, both of whom were staring at Lucy like she was an angel straight out of heaven.

He could appreciate the sentiment, but he wanted to be the only one free to gaze at her like that. The men seemed to understand his tone because they moved on after a minute.

Lucy let out a strained laugh. "It's weird to be the center of attention."

He took a long pull on his beer and kissed her forehead. "You deserve it, sweetheart. These are your adoring fans."

She stared at him, searching his face like she was trying to figure out if he meant those words. "You're not angry that people keep interrupting us to talk to me?"

He shook his head. "Are you kidding? I'm thanking my lucky stars I get to be the guy at your side tonight. I'll play second fiddle to you anytime I have the chance."

She gave him a slow smile. "I can't ever imagine you as a second fiddle, but I'm glad you followed me tonight."

He was, too. He'd spent the whole damn day thinking about her and cursing himself for how he'd acted. Of course she was looking at the ranch's finances. It's what his father had asked her to do. Derek must have misread the situation. After all, Lucy hadn't mentioned any concerns about the books to Caden. He had no reason not to trust her, despite his problems with her mother.

She gestured to the corner of the bar where her group of carolers had retreated with their men. "Should we join them?"

"It's your night, Lucy. Whatever you want."

She bit down on her lower lip as her eyes darkened, telling him without words exactly what she wanted. Heat curled through his body in response.

"I want to go home," she told him, reaching up to press her hand to the back of his neck and draw him down to her for a slow, heated kiss. "Back to the ranch," she clarified.

"Sounds like a perfect plan to me. It's still coming down hard out there, so I'll drive us back and we can get your car tomorrow once they've plowed the roads."

She nodded. "I realized on the way into town that a two-wheel drive compact isn't exactly made for winter driving."

They said goodbye to their friends and walked out into the snowy night. "Does it always snow this much in Colorado?" she asked, pulling her hat down around her ears and snuggling against Caden's side as they walked.

"Not always so consistently this early in the season," he answered, catching a few of the fluffy flakes on his gloved hand. "It's good for the ski resorts, though, and it explains why downtown Crimson has been so busy. People hear the snow is great out here, and they make plans to spend the holidays on the slopes."

"Do you ski?"

Caden nodded. "Tyson taught me the first winter I came to live with them. He was so damn fast on the mountain. I never could keep up with him."

"I'm sure you tried."

"I ate so much snow my first ski season from all the face-planting I did." He laughed softly, surprised at the fondness of his memories. Everything about his relationship with his brother had been tainted by Tyson's death. It had forced Caden to refocus his past through the lens of how he'd failed Tyson. But tonight the guilt seemed to fade away to leave nothing but happy thoughts.

Another gift Lucy gave him.

"Tyson's idea of lessons was taking me to the top of the highest peak and racing down."

"That must have been terrifying."

"We were both adrenaline junkies."

"Is that why you joined the army?"

He shrugged, no longer shocked at how easily she could read him. "Partly, I think. At that point, I also wanted something that belonged to just me."

"I understand that," she said softly.

When they got to where he'd parked the truck, he opened the passenger-side door for her, then came around and turned on the ignition.

"Do you want to learn to ski while you're here?"

She laughed. "No, thanks. The thought of strapping sticks to my feet and hurtling down a mountain is enough to make me queasy. There are plenty of other ways to get my heart racing."

"I can think of a few," he told her and leaned over the console for a kiss. He'd meant it to be only a brief embrace, a prelude for what was to come.

But when his mouth met hers, it was as if someone lit a match to a bonfire inside him. He flamed to life, and Lucy was the oxygen his fire needed to keep it raging.

She hadn't yet buckled her seat belt, so he lifted her up and over the console, into his lap.

She seemed as engulfed in incendiary need as he felt. She reached inside his coat and tugged at the shirt he'd tucked into jeans. Her clever fingers skimmed along his skin, and all he could think about was getting closer.

So much for the belief that one night would satisfy his need. He kissed her like his life depended on it, because maybe it did. He slanted his head, tangling his tongue with hers as he pressed his palms into the small of her back. Even in the crowded truck cab, she fit perfectly against him.

Hot air blasted from the dashboard vents as he took hold of her hips, pulling her even tighter against him. She moaned low in her throat, a sound that drove him wild.

Suddenly he was a teenager again, parked with a girl and wondering if there was anything more perfect than the feel of soft curves against his hard body.

A firm knock on the window made Lucy jerk away from him. Her back slammed into the steering wheel, and the blare of the horn split the quiet. She scrambled back into her seat as a light flashed in the fogged-up front window.

Caden drew in a breath and hit the button to roll down the window on the truck's driver's side.

"Howdy, folks," Marcus Pike, one of Crimson's deputy sheriffs, drawled.

"Hey, Marcus." Caden squinted and held up a hand. "Mind turning off the flashlight?"

"Sure thing, Sharpe," the older man said with a knowing smile. "I noticed your truck was running but you weren't going anywhere. It's a cold night and a lot of people are doing some preholiday celebrating. Thought I'd check and make sure everything's okay."

"Just letting her warm up before heading back to the ranch," Caden explained, patting the dashboard.

"I bet." Marcus leaned in closer and waved at Lucy. "I heard a bit of your caroling tonight, ma'am. You have a lovely voice."

She cleared her throat. "Thank you."

"It's been a few years," he said to Caden, "since you and I have found ourselves in this kind of situation, Sharpe." Marcus let his gaze slide from Caden to Lucy. "Our boy here dated my daughter when they were in high school."

Caden stifled a groan. He hadn't exactly "dated" Britney Pike, but he'd been caught with her on the ridge where local teens hung out on weekend nights.

"I heard Britney got married a couple of years ago. Living in Golden now, right?"

Marcus nodded. "About to give Jana and me our first grandbaby."

"Congratulations." Caden forced a smile. "If there's nothing else, I guess we'll be on our way."

"That work for you, ma'am?" Marcus asked Lucy, and the implication that she might not be fine with Caden made him want to roar in protest.

He'd been adopted by Garrett almost twenty years ago, but some people in Crimson refused to see him as anything but the troubled kid with the mom who'd over-dosed and no other family to step in and help raise him.

Lucy didn't seem to realize there might be an under-lying meaning in the deputy's question, or if she did, she pretended to ignore it. She reached across the con-sole and laced her fingers with Caden's. "I'm exactly where I want to be. Thanks for checking on us, Officer."

Some of the tension gripping Caden's chest loosened. "Tell your dad I said hello," Marcus said, then turned and headed back to his cruiser.

Caden shifted to face Lucy as he rolled up the win-dow, ready to apologize for putting her in that sort of situation.

Only to find her dissolving into a fit of giggles. "That was hilarious," she said, her shoulders shaking. "I feel like I'm fifteen except that never happened to me when I was a teenager. We actually got caught making out."

She pointed at Caden. "And you once had a thing with the sheriff's daughter?"

"Marcus Pike is a deputy sheriff. Cole Bennett took over the department a couple of years ago when the old sheriff retired. Cole is about—"

"Stop changing the subject." Lucy threw back her head and laughed more. "Did you have some kind of death wish as a teenager?"

"Maybe," he admitted and found himself grinning back at her. He'd had plenty of run-ins with law enforcement as a surly kid and rowdy teenager, and even though he'd done well in the army, back in Crimson his feelings about authority were mired in and convoluted by the mistakes he'd made as a youth.

As she seemed to do with every aspect of his life, Lucy changed his normal dynamic. She changed who he was and who he wanted to be. Her fingers were still intertwined with his, and he lifted her hand, turning it over to place a kiss on the inside of her wrist.

He continued to hold her hand as he drove, the truck's headlights illuminating the whirling snow and limiting his vision to only three feet in front of them.

Her phone chimed and he released her so she could pull it from her jacket pocket. "Mom says their flight out of JFK got canceled."

"I thought it wasn't scheduled until tomorrow?" he asked.

"The East Coast is getting hit with a big storm, too, so flights are already being affected. They're coming home a day later now."

"Not much time for her to plan a Christmas wedding," he muttered, wondering if Maureen had somehow orchestrated the delay to keep him away from his father until right before the big event. Realistically he knew she couldn't control the weather, but it seemed awfully convenient.

"Oh, she sent me a list of things to do so that everything's ready to go when they return."

I'm not ready, he wanted to shout but kept his mouth shut. He'd been a jerk this morning and wasn't going to be stupid enough to ruin tonight, too. It wasn't Lucy's fault his dad and her mom were stuck on the East Coast. He also couldn't make himself believe that she had any corrupt intentions where his father was concerned. In fact, it seemed as though her mother's various machinations with men had been difficult for Lucy.

She was as much a pawn in Maureen's schemes as any of them. Caden needed Garrett back on the ranch so he could truly determine if his dad's heart was in jeopardy. Garrett could say what he wanted about making his own decisions, but Caden couldn't afford to let him be hurt again.

Not that he minded a few extra days with Lucy. They hadn't talked about her plans for after the holidays, but he assumed she'd be returning to Florida. He wanted to make the most of every moment he had with her.

The thought pinged through his mind that he should ask her to stay, but he pushed it aside before it had a chance to take root. Lucy deserved a man who could love her with his whole heart, and Caden's had been too damaged over the years to be much use to anyone.

"You're still hoping your dad will call off the wedding," Lucy said quietly.

Garrett took the turn that led to the ranch, gripping the steering wheel with both hands. "I'd be happier if they didn't rush into anything."

He held his breath as he waited for her response.

"That would probably be wise, given..." She stopped, her body going stiff as if she was about to say something she shouldn't.

"Given what?" he demanded.

She turned to him and smiled, but it didn't reach her eyes. "It's been a whirlwind courtship, and your dad seems like an old-fashioned kind of guy. Mom is all about instant gratification, but sometimes waiting only makes the outcome sweeter in the end." She raised a brow. "Know what I mean?"

He actually had no idea what the hell she was talking about. But he was damn sure it wasn't what she'd meant to say in the first place.

They could deal with the reality of her mother and his father when they returned from New York. Tonight all he wanted was to hold Lucy in his arms again.

"You snore," he said instead of answering her.

He watched her mouth drop open as he parked his truck in the oversize garage bay.

"I d-do not," she stammered. "I can't believe you'd say that to me. That's like telling a woman a pair of jeans makes her butt look big."

He hopped out of the truck, walked around to her side and opened the door. "Good news. The jeans you wear make your butt look amazing." He gave her an ex-aggerated leer. "I'd say your butt is perfect no matter what you're wearing, but I better double-check to make sure. Climb down and turn around for me."

She got out of the truck and promptly shoved him in the chest. He took a step back, smiling at how flustered she appeared. "Are you trying to *not* get lucky to-night?" she demanded, flipping her long hair over one shoulder. "Because that's where you're headed pretty darn quickly."

Lucky. Wasn't that just the right word to describe how he felt with Lucy? Lucky to have his heart filled with happiness. Lucky to be the man she'd chosen, if even for a short time. "I think it's cute," he said, reaching for her.

"It's embarrassing." She sidestepped him and stalked out of the garage and toward the house. The floodlight that hung above the garage illuminated the driveway now that the snow had finally slowed.

"Be careful," he called as he hit the button to close the garage door, then followed her. "The ground will be slick in spots."

As she got close to the porch, she bent forward and grabbed a handful of snow. Before he realized what she was doing, she hurled a snowball toward him. It landed with a thunk against his chest, snow splattering everywhere.

"Nice aim," he said with a chuckle.

She gave him an arch look. "I was going for your head." She bent and formed another snowball. He ducked as it went whizzing by him, then gathered enough snow to make one of his own.

"You're in trouble now, sweetheart."

He expected her to declare game over, but as always, Lucy surprised him. "I'm going to take you down, cowboy," she shouted and ran behind the edge of the porch rail for cover.

The next few minutes were filled with shouts and laughter as they engaged in an epic snowball fight, the kind of fun Caden hadn't had since he and Tyson were kids.

He landed a few good ones, but Lucy proved to have the aim of a major-league pitcher. By the time she called a truce, he had icy water dripping down his front and back.

He held up his hands, palms forward as he moved toward her. "You win," he called.

"I don't snore," she insisted.

"Whatever you say."

She reached out a hand and brushed snow from his shoulder. Her cheeks were flushed and her eyes sparkled. She was so damn beautiful it took his breath away. "I got you good."

"You have no idea," he murmured and leaned in to kiss her.

"I like winter," she said against his mouth. "It's kind of fun."

"Everything is fun with you, Lucy."

She wound her arms around his neck. "But now I'm ready to warm up."

"I can help with that," he told her and lifted her into his arms. She wrapped her legs around his hips, and he carried her up the porch steps and into the house.

A shiver passed through her as his fingers moved under her clothes to press into her back. He walked up the stairs, careful not to bump her into a wall, and carried her down the hallway, into his bedroom.

By the time he gently put her down on the bed, her whole body trembled. "I'd like to think that's a reaction to me," he said, straightening to tug off her boots, "but you're freezing."

"May-maybe winter and I," she said through chattering teeth, "don't ge-get along so well af-after all."

"I'll be your personal space heater."

She smiled at the simple jest and something shifted in his heart. More like an unfurling, all the tender bits that he'd hidden for years advancing into the light that seemed to emanate from Lucy like a beacon. He was falling for her, fast and hard and unable or unwilling to stop the descent.

He quickly helped her undress, then shucked off his clothes, hissing out a breath as her ice-cold hands flattened on his chest. Within minutes, her shivers had subsided and they were both heated from the inside out, a tangle of limbs and sweet caresses.

It was difficult to know where he ended and Lucy began, and he'd never imagined he could feel so unfettered in joining himself to another person. He wasn't sure how he'd stand it when this finally ended. Or how to make sure it never did.

Chapter Twelve

Lucy stood in front of the Christmas tree the following afternoon, reaching out a hand to touch the tip of one of the colorful lights Caden had strung. The scent of pine filled the room, and each of the decorations she'd placed made her heart happy.

She realized she'd never appreciated the holidays at the various retail shops where she'd worked because the lights and trimmings held no meaning for her. And her mother's vacillating relationship with Christmas, going all out when she was with a man, then ignoring the holidays completely when it was just her and Lucy, had also tainted the season.

Her time in Crimson made Lucy understand how special Christmas could be. She understood that the decorations represented years of tradition, of the love between a husband and wife, a mother and son, and later the family Garrett had created with Tyson and Caden.

For the first time, Lucy wanted to create her own traditions. Caroling on a downtown corner with friends…a raucous snowball fight breaking the quiet of a December night. She pressed her fingers to her chest as her breath caught at the thought of little boys with Caden's tousled hair and mischievous smile romping through the snow.

Could that sort of life be possible for her? She'd learned the best way to avoid disappointment and heart-ache was to keep her expectations low. But Caden made her want a life she believed could make her happy.

She knew it wouldn't be easy. Even if her mother truly loved Garrett, Maureen had a tendency to sabo-tage the good things in their lives. Lucy would have to trust Caden enough to explain fully her mother's his-tory and hope that he'd understand and allow his father to make his own decisions about his life.

But she couldn't go forward until they were both on the same page about her past, the choices Maureen had made and Lucy's role in protecting her mother when re-ality got to be too much for Maureen to handle.

There was another truth she had to make Caden see first, and nerves skittered through her as she heard the front door of the house open and shut.

He appeared in the doorway a moment later, his color high from the cold. "How fast can you get ready?"

"For what?"

A small smile played at the corner of his mouth. "A date."

"With you?"

His grin widened. "Unless you have someone else in mind."

She shook her head. "Of course not. I just wasn't ex-pecting… I hadn't planned…"

"New plan." He stepped forward, lifted her hand to his mouth. "I'd like to take you out on a real date, Lucy. Something special. Will you go with me?"

"Yes," she whispered, the weight of the conversation she'd planned to have with him lifting momentarily. They had time to discuss the serious bits later.

She wanted to believe what she had to tell him wouldn't change things between them, but there was no doubt it would cast a shadow on their night. Now that she'd become accustomed to basking in the light of her feelings for him, she wasn't ready to risk giving the darkness an opening.

She took a quick shower and got ready, borrowing a dark green sweater dress from her mother's closet. It had long sleeves and fell almost to her knees, so it would be appropriate for December, but the deep V of both the neckline and back added a pinch of sexiness to the outfit.

She'd packed one pair of high heels, black and strappy, and slipped her feet into them, loving the tiny bows at the ankles. After curling her hair and adding a bit of mascara and lip gloss, she spritzed herself with perfume and turned to the full-length mirror that hung on the closet door.

The dress was gorgeous, but was it appropriate for whatever Caden had planned? They were still in Colorado in December. He'd said "special," but for all Lucy knew, that meant a hoedown at the local lodge.

"You're the most beautiful thing I've ever seen."

She whirled around at the sound of Caden's deep voice. He stood in the doorway, wearing a dark sports jacket with a crisp white shirt, burgundy tie and pair of navy trousers. A wide-brimmed Western hat was perched on his head, and she'd never seen her high-mountain cowboy look more handsome.

"Thank you," she said, "but I think you need to get out more."

He shook his head. "I've been all over the world. You're it for me."

It felt as though her heart skipped a beat. She knew he was talking about how she looked, but she had trouble not reading more into the words. The way he said them, his tone filled with awe, made her feel like he was choosing her, and nothing had ever meant so much.

"You look quite handsome yourself," she said, making her voice light. No sense in letting him see how far gone she was. Not until she was certain he felt the same way. "Cowboy couture suits you."

"Cowboy couture," he repeated with a chuckle. "Is that official retail lingo?"

She moved toward him. "That's officially me giving you a compliment." She tipped up her chin and kissed him. With the heels on, she didn't need to go up on her toes, although he was still a couple of inches taller than her. He took her hand and led her down the stairs to the front of the house.

"I'm going to pull the truck to the front porch so you don't twist an ankle in those shoes walking across the snow."

She made a face. "I forgot about the snow. I could change into—"

"Hell, no," he interrupted. "Your shoes are the stuff of my wildest fantasies. You can keep them on all night." He leaned in and nipped at her earlobe. "Maybe later we'll negotiate you wearing the shoes and nothing else."

She sighed. "What do I get in the deal?"

"Whatever you want."

You, she wanted to shout. *I want you.*

Her heart pitched at the thought, and she pushed away. "I need to check on Cocoa and the puppies. I'll be out in a minute."

The dog wagged her tail and looked up at Lucy when she came into the laundry room. Thankfully, there'd been no more talk about moving Cocoa to the barn. The puppies were tiny but they were beginning to gain weight and size. "I've got a date with a hot cowboy tonight, Cocoa. Wish me luck."

The dog yawned and turned to lick the smallest pup. Lucy still hated that they hadn't been able to save the last puppy, but Cocoa didn't seem to feel the loss. She had her hands full with her six wriggling bundles.

"You've got more important things to worry about than my love life. I'll see you when we get back, sweet girl."

She slipped into her coat and opened the front door. A gust of frigid air whipped across her bare legs, and for a moment she rethought her decision to wear the dress with no tights. But then she remembered the look in Caden's eyes when his gaze had swept over her. A minute of cold was definitely worth his reaction.

He was waiting on the porch, and took her hand as she walked out. "I can make it to the truck," she told him with a laugh.

"Give me some credit." He placed his other hand on the small of her back. "I'm trying to be a gentleman. It's new for me."

She laughed and allowed him to lead her down the steps and help her into the truck.

"Where are we going?" she asked when he turned out of the driveway in the opposite direction of downtown Crimson.

"Aspen."

Of course Lucy had heard of the ritzy ski town, but she'd never imagined going on a date there. When she'd first come to Crimson, her only purpose had been to protect her mother's relationship with Garrett.

In the course of almost two weeks, the town had become her home. She had more of a life here than she'd made in a decade living in Florida. She was so grateful for everything she'd experienced and couldn't wait to have a night out with Caden. In some strange way, it felt as though this night made what was between them official.

"You know you don't have to try to impress me," she said quietly, keeping her gaze trained on the guardrail at the edge of the highway. "I'm a sure thing."

"Don't make yourself less than who you are, Lucy."

The words were spoken gently, but they felt like a slap to the face.

"I'm not," she insisted.

"Yes, you are." He reached for her hand, but she pulled away, embarrassed that he could read her so easily. "Even though we started off unconventionally—"

"Because you hated me," she muttered.

"I didn't trust you," he clarified. "But now I know who you are, and I want you to see yourself the way I do. I want to woo you. I want you to understand you deserve every good thing. You deserve to be cherished."

I deserve to be loved.

She clasped a hand over her mouth and turned to Caden, afraid she'd spoken out loud her most secret desire.

"You don't have to agree with me," he said, and she could tell by his relaxed manner that she'd only thought that last bit. Thank goodness. "But I hope you can allow yourself to enjoy the night. I know I plan to have a hell of a time."

"I can't wait for whatever you have planned," she said honestly.

What he had planned turned out to be dinner at one of the fanciest restaurants in Aspen. La Bonne Maison was an elegant, French-inspired bistro she'd seen mentioned in the tabloids because of its popularity with the celebrities who flocked to Aspen during the ski season.

"This place is famous," she whispered as he pulled to a stop at the curb and a uniformed valet immediately opened her door.

She climbed out of the truck and almost gasped as one of her favorite actresses walked past her and into the restaurant.

Caden took her hand, squeezing gently.

She knew she was gaping but couldn't stop herself. "That was—"

"I know," he said quietly. "Aspen is full of Hollywood types, especially during the holidays."

"You don't seem impressed."

He shrugged. "You impress me. I bet Ms. A-List Actress couldn't assist a cantankerous dog through a difficult birth without freaking out."

"Cocoa is not cantankerous," Lucy countered as Caden led her forward. A doorman opened the heavy wooden front door and they walked into the space, with its dark paneled walls and oversize fireplace that took up one whole wall. The lighting of the restaurant was soft, giving it an intimate feel. A woman greeted Caden at the hostess stand, air-kissing each of his cheeks before turning to Lucy.

"Welcome to La Bonne Maison," she said in a heavy French accent. "I'm so happy Caden finally had a reason to accept my offer."

"I'm excited to be here. As far as your offer…" Lucy threw a questioning glance toward Caden.

"Louisa owns La Bonne Maison. I helped match her with her dog," he explained almost sheepishly.

"Jacques is the best companion I've ever had," the woman said with a nod. "Far more agreeable than my ex-husband. I've wanted to thank Caden with a special dinner, but apparently he's never had a reason to dine with us until you."

Caden cleared his throat, appearing uncomfortable at the restaurant owner's comments. "The ranch keeps me busy," he muttered.

"*Oui, mon chéri.* But you must make time for the joie de vivre." She took Lucy's hand. "This one has finally helped you to see that."

"*Oui,*" Caden agreed in an exaggerated accent, making Lucy smile.

Louisa led them to a small booth that afforded both privacy and a view of the rest of the patrons. "Our best table," Louisa explained. "Mariah was not pleased…" She shrugged. "But c'est la vie."

When she walked away, Lucy leaned across the table. "That must be one incredible dog."

Caden grinned. "He's a good fit for her."

"Thank you for taking me here," Lucy said after a waiter had brought a bottle of wine and poured two glasses.

He arched a brow. "My father isn't the only one who can wine and dine a woman."

A tendril of unease snaked along Lucy's spine. "I

don't want you to think I need to be wined and dined. I'm not my mother."

Caden set his wineglass on the table and took her hand. "I know that, but I wanted to share this night with you. It's about us, Lucy. No one else."

As was his way, Caden seemed to know exactly what to say to put her mind at ease. Her body relaxed and she smiled at him. "Then let's have the most amazing evening. Just us."

"Don't even tell me my snoring woke you up."

Caden smiled as he crawled back under the covers the next morning. "Working a ranch woke me up," he said, dropping a kiss on her bare shoulder. "But all I could think about was the image of you warm and naked in my bed."

She gave a little yelp as his cold fingers brushed the curve of her waist. "You've already been out?"

"It's almost eight, sleepyhead."

She turned to him, wrapping a leg around his hip and making his body pound with need. As beautiful as she'd looked last night in her fancy dress and heels, she was even lovelier with no makeup and her hair tumbling over the pillow. "Someone kept me awake all night. I was catching up on sleep. Are you playing hooky this morning?"

"For an hour or so," he answered. "Chad is going to work on the fence line near the edge of the west pasture. I'll catch up with him later."

"Then we'd better make the most of this hour," she whispered and snuggled closer.

They both laughed as her stomach gave a low growl.

"You've been in bed too long," he said, kissing her hair. "It's time for breakfast."

"I can make something easy," she told him, keeping the sheet tucked around her gorgeous breasts. "If you need to get back to work…"

"No sense playing hooky if I don't make the most of it." He pulled a navy Henley over his head. "How do you like your eggs?"

"However you make them."

"Butter or jelly on the toast?"

She smiled. "Butter *and* jelly."

"Got it." He smoothed a strand of hair away from her face and kissed her again. "Breakfast in fifteen minutes."

"I could grow accustomed to the service around here," she told him.

He winked. "I sure hope so." He moved toward the kitchen, passing his father's bedroom near the top of the staircase. He'd gotten a text early this morning that Garrett and Maureen were rebooked on a flight that would arrive in Denver tomorrow morning. Caden wasn't sure what that would mean for his relationship with Lucy, but he knew he couldn't imagine saying goodbye to her now.

He had no doubt they'd have to get creative with their time together. Caden thought about how he might fix up the small guesthouse situated to the south of the barn. Would Lucy want to get her own apartment in town if she was going to stay in Crimson?

Could he ask her to stay beyond the holidays? Garrett had always told him Christmas was the time for new beginnings, but Caden never had a reason to believe it since he'd first come to live on Sharpe Ranch, until Lucy.

He started frying bacon in a pan on the stove, then chopped vegetables and cracked eggs into a mixing bowl to make omelets.

By the time Lucy appeared in the kitchen, her hair damp and in a loose bun at the back of her neck, he was plating the food. She sat a stack of files on the table and slipped into a seat.

"You're an amazing cook," she said around a bite of omelet. "How am I ever going to go back to cold cereal for breakfast?"

"Don't," he replied immediately and wasn't sure which one of them was more shocked by the word. "Stay in Crimson," he said before he lost his nerve. "Stay with me."

She studied his face, as if searching for something to help her know how to answer. "Caden, I want to say yes."

He sat down across from her. "Then say yes."

"I need to talk to you about something before we go any further." She pushed her plate to the side and grabbed one of the file folders.

"That sounds ominous," he said with a smile that she didn't return. His stomach clenched when she opened the folder to reveal the spreadsheets and ledgers he recognized from the ranch's finances.

"Derek Lawson is stealing from you," she said, then swallowed hard. "I know he was your brother's friend—"

"Tyson's best friend," Caden clarified, shock and disbelief coursing through him. "Like one of the family."

Her chest rose and fell like she couldn't draw in

enough air, but her gaze never left his. "He's skimming money from Garrett's accounts, Caden. I can prove—"

He stood up so suddenly his chair upended, landing on the floor with a clatter. "He warned me you'd do this."

Lucy's dark eyes widened. "He *warned* you?"

"He told me you called him and made some veiled accusations that—"

"I called him to see if he could explain the way he'd been keeping the books. Of course he got defensive because he's taking advantage of Sharpe Ranch and your dad's other businesses."

Caden paced to the counter, unable to look at her a moment longer. He gripped the edge of the granite until his knuckles turned white. "I bet you have a plan for getting things back on track," he said through clenched teeth.

"I have a few ideas," she agreed. "But first you need to confront Derek. He needs to admit—"

"No." Caden whirled around and stalked to the table. He couldn't allow himself to consider that Derek had betrayed him. Caden had been the one to recommend Tyson's old friend when Garrett needed help with the finances. If Derek was the villain here, it was once again Caden's fault for allowing him into their lives. He had to believe Lucy was lying.

She got out of her seat as he came toward her, not backing down for a moment. "You need to admit that this was your end game the entire time," he said.

He grabbed her arms and pulled her close enough that he could clearly see the flecks of gold around the edges of her brown eyes. "You and your mother planned the whole thing."

"Take your hands off me," she whispered, and he immediately let her go. Guilt warred with frustration inside him as she rubbed her hands against her skin where he'd held her.

Even now he wanted to put aside all of his anger and draw her to him, continue to pretend that neither of them had a history that would make what was between them impossible. "How would I have planned for someone to steal from you? I didn't even know about Derek when I came to Crimson."

"But you knew that my dad had lots of money. Your mom knows how to pick the ones with deep pockets, right?"

Lucy narrowed her eyes but didn't contradict him, only fueling his temper.

"Derek warned me you were scheming to get your hands on Garrett's money. His guess was that your mom set you up to review the books and find fault with his methods."

"I find fault with him ripping you off," she insisted.

"You're lying. This is a con."

The color drained from her face at his accusation. "How can you believe that after everything that's happened between us?"

He crossed his arms over his chest and lifted a brow. "What's really happened, Lucy? Great sex? A couple of canned Christmas adventures? Did you stage the whole thing?"

She opened her mouth to argue, but the doorbell rang at that moment. Caden wanted to ignore it, but Sharpe Ranch didn't get many unannounced visitors. It could be something important. "We're not done here," he said as he turned away and moved toward the front of the house.

"Oh, yes, we are," she shouted after him.

He opened the door to reveal a tall beach-bum-type man, probably in his midfifties, with sandy blond hair and blue eyes framed by deeply tanned skin. He wore board shorts and a bulky down coat.

"You lost?"

"I'm looking for Reenie," the man said, trying to peer over Caden's shoulder. "She's not returning my calls."

"There's no one—"

"Bobby?" Lucy asked from behind him. "What are you doing here?"

"Your mom won't let up with the divorce papers, Luce. She flew me out to Colorado in the middle of winter, and now she's blowing me off."

Caden was so shocked at the man's words, he automatically took a step back.

Bobby used the opportunity to blow past Caden, heading straight for Lucy, who was now white as a ghost. "I told her the last time she can't get rid of me that easily." He wagged an angry finger in her face. "I'm not some old toy to be thrown in the trash."

"She doesn't love you, Bobby. Let her go."

"Not until she makes it worth my while. Her new man might think he can scare me off, but we both know better than that." He grabbed Lucy by the shoulders. "Talk to her, Luce."

She tried to shift away but the man held tight. "Don't touch her," Caden said.

"Dude, stay out of this. Lucy and I have got some business. Then I'll be on my way."

"You'll be on your way now." Caden grabbed the man's arm and twisted it behind his back.

Bobby let out a grunt, but his reflexes were slow, and Caden had him out into the cold morning before he could put up a decent fight.

He slammed shut the door and turned to Lucy. "I suppose you have an explanation for that, too?"

"You have to understand." She shook her head. "Mom told me she'd handle Bobby."

"So you knew she was ready to commit bigamy with my father?" The duplicity of that cut deep.

A tear tracked down Lucy's cheek as she squeezed her eyes shut. "She wouldn't have let it get that far."

"Right. It's all becoming clear now. I'm guessing Bobby is what ruined things with your mom's last boy-friend. Your mother and her not-so-ex-husband?"

"You have to believe me, Caden. She really loves your dad. I can hear it in her voice. She's different this time."

"Give me a break. The only thing that's different is that I ignored my gut when I should have trusted it. I knew you were trouble from the start. She brought you here to target me."

"No." She swiped a hand across her cheek. "She asked me to talk to you, but that was it."

"The sex was your idea of clinching the deal, then. Should I be flattered?"

"Stop making what we have into something ugly."

"We don't have *anything*."

She bit down on her lip, then whispered, "I love you, Caden. I know you feel—"

"No more." He reached her in two long strides but didn't touch her. Couldn't touch her without fear he'd lose his mind. Like he'd already lost his heart. "You know nothing about me or how I feel, so let me en-lighten you."

He leaned in and she stumbled back a step. "I don't feel anything but disgust for you and your mother. You can damn well bet I'm going to do everything in my power to make sure my father sees your mother for the gold-digging grifter she truly is. There will be *no* marriage. I can promise you that."

"They're happy together."

"Until she breaks his heart."

"She won't," Lucy argued, but there was no heat behind it. "I'll make sure she doesn't."

"And I'm going to make sure you both are out of our lives. For good."

She closed her eyes as if it was too painful to look at him and, once again, Caden wanted to pull her to him. Instead he stalked out of the house toward the barn, welcoming the cold as it matched his frozen heart. He'd forgotten to grab a coat, so he pulled one from the office and climbed in his truck to check the fence line at the edge of the property.

He wasn't sure how his life had gone to hell so quickly, but right now he needed to get away from Lucy and the thought of her betrayal.

Even though he'd known better than to open his heart, he'd done it for her. Now his chest ached like it had been cut open. He wished he could remove the throbbing organ and get rid of it forever because he knew it would never mend from this pain.

Chapter Thirteen

"You can stay here as long as you want."

Lucy sniffed as Erin handed her a bowl of ice cream later that night. She tried to force a smile but the corners of her mouth refused to pull up.

"I don't want to be in the way, especially during the holidays." She gestured to the Christmas tree set up in one corner of the cozy family room. "I must be ruining whatever plans you and David had for tonight."

After the argument with Caden that morning, Lucy had packed her bags and left Sharpe Ranch. How could she possibly face him again knowing what he believed about her?

Maybe she understood his initial reaction to what she'd told him, especially if Derek Lawson had already planted the seeds of doubt in his mind. Lucy often had misgivings about her mother's motivations regarding men, but there was something about the way she talked about Garrett that made Lucy believe this time it was different. Real.

It had been real for Lucy. That's why it hurt so badly when Caden hadn't been willing to even hear her out. Now all she had was a heart that was truly broken.

"The bar is crazy busy with people in town for the holidays, so David and I don't have plans." Erin dropped onto the couch next to Lucy. "Today was the last day of school before winter break, so all I want to do is relax and watch sappy Christmas movies. It's good to have company for the night."

Lucy let out a watery laugh. "I'm terrible company right now."

"He'll come to his senses," Erin said quietly.

Lucy had wandered in and out of the shops in downtown Crimson most of the afternoon, watching people select last-minute Christmas presents for family and friends. She'd gotten more depressed with each passing minute, hating the fact that she'd opened herself to Caden and actually believed she might finally have a chance at love.

She'd tried calling and texting her mom, but Maureen hadn't responded to any of her messages. Her makeshift plan had been to check in to one of the local hotels until she'd run into Erin coming out of Life Is Sweet.

Erin had asked the innocuous question "How's it going," prompting Lucy to burst into fat, messy tears. Without missing a beat, Erin had wrapped her in a tight hug, then led her through the front of the bakery to the commercial kitchen, where Katie Crawford was just taking a pan of muffins out of one of the big ovens.

The two women had comforted Lucy, plying her with muffins and hot tea until she'd felt marginally better. She'd been through plenty of disappointment in her life and never realized how much having friends to support her could help make the pain more manageable.

"I think he's already made his decision." Lucy wiped her nose on her sleeve, not caring that she must look like a total wreck. "I feel like he's been waiting for a reason to prove to both of us that we could never work." She took a big bite of ice cream but missed her mouth. The spoonful of chocolate ice cream landed in the middle of her chest then rolled down the front of her gray sweatshirt. "I'm a mess," she whispered as fresh tears streamed down her cheeks.

"Oh, sweetie." Erin hurried to the kitchen, grabbed a paper towel from the roll hanging under the counter, then returned and picked the glob of chocolate off Lucy's stomach. "You're not a…" She paused, a pained look on her face. "We've all been where you are right now."

Lucy shook her head. "You've been red faced and blotchy with no place to go and chocolate all over your shirtfront?"

Katie gave a small laugh. "I didn't actually mean literally. I was talking about heartbroken."

"I should have known not to fall for him." Lucy placed the dish of ice cream on the coffee table, unable to stomach any more sugar. She'd never been much of a drinker, but she could make a career as a professional emotional eater. "He told me the first time we met that he'd hurt me." She hugged her arms around her waist.

"Caden doesn't have much experience letting down his defenses. He really cares about you, Lucy."

"Not anymore."

"You can't just turn off emotions like that."

"He did."

"I don't believe it. He's upset. He blamed himself for Tyson's death and became too focused on protecting Garrett after the accident. I think he was terrified of losing the only other person who really loves him."

"I loved him," Lucy whispered.

Erin arched a brow. "Past tense?"

"I still love him, because I'm the biggest fool on the planet. It doesn't matter, anyway."

"Of course it does. Give him time. To admit that Derek is stealing from Sharpe Ranch would mean that Caden failed to protect his dad. I'm not sure he could stand that."

"But it isn't his fault."

"I know that and you know that, but it's how his mind works. Why do you think he takes in all those unwanted animals? He's a rescuer. And Garrett is important because of how he once rescued Caden from that horrible foster care situation."

"You know him well," Lucy murmured.

Erin shrugged. "I was a shy kid so I did a lot of watching the people around me. I notice things." She smiled softly. "Caden was always so big and scary in school. I think he liked the reputation he had as a bad boy. He liked people being afraid of him. But when I was a freshman and he was a sophomore, I saw him sneaking behind the bleachers of the football field by himself every day during his lunch period and after school. I might have been shy, but I was always too curious for my own good."

A laugh bubbled up in Lucy's throat. "There's curious and there's having a death wish. Weren't you scared of what you'd find?"

Erin leaned in closer. "It was a nest of baby squirrels. I think the mom had died or deserted them, and Caden was hand-feeding them."

"Why didn't he just take them home to the ranch?"

"Maybe he thought Garrett wouldn't let him keep them. But after that, I knew his rough exterior hid a soft heart. I'm sure he thought I was crazy because I smiled and waved at him every chance I got from then on. He's built a lot of walls around his heart over the years, but the goodness inside him hasn't changed."

"The fact that I love him isn't enough. He doesn't trust me, and he doesn't trust my mom." Lucy shrugged. "Half the time I don't trust her, so I should have known better than to get involved with him. My mom always manages to land on her feet no matter what life throws at her. I'm more a face-plant-on-the-ground sort of girl."

She stood and walked to the window, looking out at the quaint neighborhood of historic bungalows decorated with colored lights. This Christmas was supposed to be different, but here she was, alone again.

"He'll be back to the house by now," she said, more to herself than Erin. "He must realize I'm gone."

"Did you leave a note?" Erin asked.

"No. A clean break is better for both of us."

"It doesn't have to be a break," Erin insisted, conviction lacing her gentle tone.

"Yes, it does." Lucy blinked away another round of tears. *No more crying.* "Caden made that quite clear, and I'm not going to beg anyone for a second chance."

If there was one thing she knew how to do, it was move on with her life.

"Are you drunk?"

"Go away, Chad. What I do on my time is none of your damn business." Caden went to slam the door in the young ranch hand's face, but his hand didn't connect with the wood, so instead he lost his balance and stumbled into the wall.

Chad stepped into the house, shutting the door behind him. "You drink over half that?" he asked, pointing to the bottle of whiskey on the coffee table.

Caden righted himself and tried to focus, but the edges of his vision remained blurry. "Maybe," he muttered, narrowing his eyes. "You want a glass?"

"Where's Lucy?" Suspicion laced Chad's tone.

"You're asking a crap ton of questions tonight." Caden walked toward his empty glass of whiskey, cursing under his breath as his shin hit the edge of the table.

"Are you going to answer any of them?"

"Another question." Caden pointed to the overstuffed leather chair on the opposite side of the coffee table. "Have a seat and a drink."

Chad whistled under his breath but moved to the wet bar, pulling a shot glass out of the cabinet. Caden handed him the whiskey bottle but made a noise of reproach when Chad poured only a finger of amber liquid into the glass.

"Who's the party pooper now?" Caden demanded.

"It's called pacing myself, buddy." Chad lifted his drink in mock salute. "You should try it."

Caden grabbed the whiskey bottle and tipped it up to his lips, not bothering with his glass. "I'm celebrating tonight."

"I can't wait to hear about the occasion."

"I dodged a bullet today." Caden smiled even though it felt like his insides were ripping apart as he said the lie out loud.

"Care to elaborate?"

"I got duped by the wrong kind of woman once already and paid dearly for my mistake. We all did. It cost Tyson his life."

Chad dropped into the leather chair and ran a hand through his blond hair. "Not this again."

"You're right." Caden pointed a finger at Chad but had a hard time zeroing in on him since the young ranch hand appeared to have two heads. Maybe Chad was right and Caden should stop drinking. Instead, he took another long pull on the whiskey bottle. "Never again will I allow myself to be led around by the—"

"Where's Lucy?" Chad asked, sitting forward. "I have a bad feeling you were an idiot today."

"I've been an idiot." Caden shook his head, then stopped abruptly when the room began to spin. "Today Lucy Renner revealed her true nature to me."

Chad rolled his eyes. "And how'd she do that?"

"I'm glad you asked." He rubbed a hand across his jaw but couldn't exactly feel his face at the moment. "She accused Derek of stealing from Sharpe Ranch."

He studied Chad for a reaction, but the cowboy just stared at him.

"Did you hear me?"

"I did." Chad nodded. "I have to say it doesn't surprise me."

"Are you joking?" Caden tried to lurch to his feet but landed back on the couch with a thump. "Derek was Tyson's best friend. My dad trusted him to help with the finances because he's like family. He'd never take advantage of us that way."

"Derek was jealous of Tyson. Always had been."

"Not true," Caden argued.

"My sister dated Derek in high school. I was a few years younger but I remember her complaining that he was obsessed with beating Tyson at everything."

"Your sister also dated Tyson," Caden said quietly.

"Yeah," he agreed. "After she broke up with Derek. I don't think that went over too well, either."

Caden narrowed his eyes. "Are you saying you believe Lucy?"

"Did she have proof?"

"I don't know," Caden admitted. "I shut her down before she had a chance to explain much to me."

"I have an even worse feeling now." Chad took a deep breath and asked, "How'd you shut her down?"

"I accused her of framing Derek so she and her mother could get to Garrett's money."

Chad let out a long groan. "Dude."

"What?" Caden demanded, suddenly feeling far more sober than he should have based on the amount of alcohol he'd consumed tonight. "Her mother has a history."

He stabbed at the air with one finger. "Hell, Maureen isn't even divorced from her last husband, who showed up here in the middle of my argument with Lucy. How do you like that little twist? Maureen Renner is willing to do anything to get what she wants. And Lucy knew about the husband. She doesn't—"

"Have you talked to your dad?"

Caden opened his mouth to answer then shut it again.

"Seriously?" Chad asked. "Don't you think you should figure out what Garrett knows before you make assumptions about the situation?"

"Of course he doesn't know," Caden said, blinking.

"He's not stupid, Caden. He was a wreck after Tyson died, but you weren't much better. He's got things under control. He met Maureen and fell in love with her, but he can take care of himself. If she has skeletons in her closet, I bet he knows they're there."

Caden shook his head. "He's not the same man as he was before the accident."

"Are you?"

"I don't matter."

"Tell that to your dad." Chad lifted his glass to his lips and drained it, then set it back on the table with a thunk. "Tell that to Lucy."

But Caden couldn't tell Lucy anything because...

"She's gone."

"Gone where?"

Caden lifted a brow. "She packed her bags and took off."

"Did you call her?"

"Why would I call her?"

Chad held out his hands, palms up. "To apologize for being an idiot?"

"You don't know that she's right about Derek."

"You don't know that she's wrong."

"I do..." Caden stopped midsentence as his stomach filled with bitter acid. The truth was, he didn't know anything. He'd made assumptions about Lucy and her mother based on what had happened to him—the way he'd been deceived and hurt. He should have known better than anyone that people's pasts didn't define them.

If that were the case, Garrett and Tyson would have never invited him into their home. He never would have had a family of his own. He'd made so many damned mistakes in his life, and there was a good chance the biggest one had been this morning when he'd hurt Lucy.

"It's actually good to know," Chad said as he stood, "that you're as human as the rest of us."

Caden glanced up, trying to focus on Chad's words over the pounding in his head. "What the hell is that supposed to mean?"

"Around here you're superhuman. You get up earlier than anyone else and work later. Hell, you even rescue unwanted animals. As far as Garrett is concerned, you can do no wrong."

Chad held up a hand when Caden was about to argue. "It sucked that Tyson died. There's no two ways about it. But it wasn't your fault, and everyone seems to know that except you. Your dad lost one son. Don't you think you owe it to him to let go of your guilt and be happy? That's all he wants, Caden."

"I'm happy," Caden lied.

"Lucy made you happy," Chad said. "I'm not a rocket scientist, but I'm smart enough to know that if a woman like her chose me, I'd do anything in my power to make sure I didn't screw it up."

He walked toward the front door, then turned back to Caden. "I get that loyalty is a big deal to you, but take another look at Derek. He might not be the friend you believe he is. And Lucy definitely isn't the enemy here, Caden."

Caden sat back against the couch cushions as the front door opened and closed. He swallowed against the bitterness rising in his throat. Was Chad right? Had he made a mistake in doubting Lucy? He'd been so sure he had a handle on things.

But the truth was his feelings for her scared the hell out of him, and in some ways having an excuse to push her away had been easier than really giving what was between the two of them a shot. She'd left him, but as much as that hurt, he could only imagine how much worse it would be if he'd admitted he loved her.

Oh, hell. He loved her.

He tipped back his head and the room started to spin again, matching the emotions swirling inside him. He closed his eyes, hoping to make everything go away, especially the mess he'd created for himself and the pain he'd caused the woman he loved.

Lucy slammed the trunk of her rental car shut the next afternoon and then turned to Erin.

"Have a wonderful Christmas," she said cheerily, pasting on a bright smile.

Erin's eyes gentled and Lucy knew she wasn't fooling her friend with her chipper tone.

"You should stay," Erin told her gently.

Lucy shook her head. "It's time for me to leave Crimson. My mom doesn't need me like she thinks she does. Garrett clearly loves her. As much as I'll miss you and the other ladies, this isn't my place. I can't go back to the ranch, and without that…"

"I'm still shocked that Caden hasn't come to his senses and reached out to you."

"Clearly Caden said everything he needed to me the other morning."

"But you can't spend Christmas alone," Erin insisted.

Lucy shrugged. "It won't be the first time, and at this point I just need to get home." Her voice cracked on the last word, and she pressed her lips together. During her short time in Crimson, this town had started to feel like home. Sharpe Ranch felt like home. Caden had become her home.

But that had all been an illusion, wishful thinking on her part.

"My plan is to stay the night in Albuquerque. If I make good time on the drive, I should reach Memphis by tomorrow. Maybe I'll spend Christmas at Graceland this year."

Erin looked past Lucy to the clouds gathering over Crimson Mountain. "The snow is going to get worse. You should at least wait until the storm passes."

Lucy glanced at her watch. "I don't know what's going on with my mom's phone, but Garrett texted that they made it to Denver and are on their way home. I want to be far enough away when they get to Crimson that she can't expect me to come back to the ranch. It's too difficult to think about facing Caden again."

"I'm going to have some words with that man," Erin told her.

"No." Lucy gave Erin a quick hug. "He's just trying to protect his dad."

"You're not the bad guy."

"I hope he realizes that someday."

Erin grabbed her hand and squeezed. "Are you sure you won't stay?"

"He hasn't given me a reason to," she said, pulling away.

"Be safe on the drive. Cell service is spotty until you get over the pass. Text or call when you're on the other side."

"I will." After a final hug, Lucy started on her way. As if on cue, the snow fell heavier as she turned onto the highway that led out of town. She patted the tiny car's dashboard, saying a silent prayer that the roads remained drivable until she was over Crimson Mountain.

Her initial plan had been to wait and leave after the forecast storm, but she had a vague premonition of being stranded in Crimson and her mother forcing another confrontation with Caden.

As much as she loved her mom and wanted to believe her feelings for Garrett were true, Caden hadn't been wrong in his assessment of Maureen's romantic history. The fact that Bobby Santino had shown up at the ranch and was probably still hanging around town didn't help matters.

No, she had to get out now.

There was only so much rejection she could withstand at one time. She needed to begin the difficult process of rebuilding her life and mending her broken heart. What other choice did she have?

Chapter Fourteen

Caden pulled out his cell and punched in Lucy's number, then hit Cancel before placing the call. He'd done the same thing so many times throughout the day, he was surprised he hadn't worn an indentation into the phone's touch screen.

But not once had he actually let the call go through. He didn't know what the hell he'd say if she actually picked up. He'd woken early with a Rocky Mountain–sized headache. After a morning spent in one of the far pastures, he'd come into the house and flipped open the files Lucy had left on the kitchen table.

The accounting side of the business had never been his responsibility, but he looked for discrepancies or ledger entries that would give him some clue as to the truth of what was happening with the Sharpe Ranch finances.

When he heard the front door open late in the afternoon, he sprang up, hope blooming that Lucy had returned and they could work things out.

Instead, he found his dad and Maureen in the farmhouse's entry, both hauling in giant suitcases.

"You didn't leave with that much stuff," he said by way of greeting.

Garrett gave a hearty laugh. "We had to buy new luggage in the city just to manage our haul for the way home."

"Your father is quite the shopper," Maureen said, grinning at him.

"Right," Caden muttered, then felt his mouth drop open as Garrett's eyes lit with excitement.

"Those salespeople couldn't keep up with me," he said with a laugh. "We're going to have one helluva Christmas this year, son." He turned to Maureen and gave her a smacking kiss on the lips. "I can't remember when I had so damn much fun."

Maybe he hadn't realized it before, but Caden was suddenly struck by how happy his dad looked. Color was high on his cheeks and his blue eyes sparkled with joy.

"Where's Lucy?" Maureen asked, pulling a small paper bag out of her purse. "I found something for her in the airport. She used to collect snow globes, so I—"

"She's gone," Caden said tightly.

Erin MacDonald had texted him last night with the message that Lucy was staying in town with her. At least he knew she was safe and with a friend, but he wasn't ready to share that with Maureen. If Lucy had wanted her mother to know where she was, he figured she would have called her.

Garrett took off his canvas jacket and hung it on the coat hook next to the door. "When will she be back? The four of us should go into town for dinner tonight."

Caden's stomach clenched at the question he had no idea how to answer. "I don't think she's coming back."

Maureen's finely arched brows drew together. "What happened?" She took a step toward Caden. "What did you do?"

"Let him explain, darlin'." Garrett placed a hand on Maureen's arm.

"I think *you* need to explain," Caden told Maureen, letting yesterday's anger surge back into his veins. "Maybe you want to explain to my father why your not-so-ex-husband paid a visit to the ranch and Lucy accused a longtime family friend of stealing from the ranch."

Maureen's mouth dropped open. "Bobby was here?"

"I told you I didn't think my message to him went through on the plane," Garrett said, shaking his head. "I hope he didn't give you and Lucy any trouble, Caden."

"What message?" Caden demanded.

"I told him I need to reschedule our meeting for today."

Caden pointed between his father and Maureen. "You already know she's still married?"

"I wanted to keep it a secret and try to handle Bobby myself," Maureen admitted. "But that didn't work out so well in the past. Lucy convinced me to share the truth with your father."

Garrett took a step forward, and Caden was reminded of all the times he'd been lectured for making stupid decisions as a teenager. "You knew I asked Lucy to review the finances. I needed someone unbiased to confirm my suspicions about Derek."

Caden ran a hand through his hair, a sick pit opening in his stomach. "Suspicions?"

"I could tell something wasn't right with the way he was handling the books. His monthly reports had discrepancies that made no sense. But he was a supposed friend of your brother's and you seemed to trust him implicitly. I didn't want to accuse him without having proof."

"Lucy truly is a whiz with numbers. They trusted her with everything at the store in Florida—at least, until I got involved." Maureen shook her head, obviously regretting the difficulties she'd caused her daughter.

Caden cursed under his breath. "Derek convinced me that Lucy and Maureen were trying to frame him so they could get access to your money."

Garrett's eyes narrowed. "That son of a—"

"I love your father," Maureen said, taking Garrett's hand in hers. "I understand you had your doubts when I came to Crimson, and I hoped spending time with Lucy would show you I couldn't be the woman you first thought. Not with Lucy in my corner. She's truly the best part of me."

"I said awful things to her," Caden said quietly, hating himself for what an ass he'd been. But not half as much as he imagined Lucy hated him right now.

"I raised you better than that," Garrett said sharply.

"Damn it, I was trying to protect you. I've failed everyone I ever loved, and I wasn't going to fail you again."

Caden couldn't stand the sorrow in his father's eyes. He couldn't help but believe he'd put it there.

"You've never failed me," Garrett whispered.

Caden wanted to run away, like he had as a boy after his mother had died. Like he had from the first foster home social services had dropped him into. And the second. And the third. But it was time both he and Garrett faced the truth of what he'd done. It was the only way he'd ever move forward. "I let Tyson die."

Garrett took a step back, as if Caden had slapped him. "You don't believe that. You can't."

"Why not?" Caden threw up his hands. "It's the truth. If I'd been there, I might have reached him in time."

Garrett squeezed his eyes shut, his barrel chest rising and falling. Caden noticed that he never let go of Maureen's hand. In fact, Garrett pulled her closer as if drawing strength from having her next to him.

Caden realized that's how he'd felt about Lucy when they were together, and another wave of regret washed over him.

"Tyson was killed on impact," his dad said in a dull tone. "You talked to the search-and-rescue commander. We both read the report."

"But I—"

"It was an accident, Caden. A horrible, tragic accident. The only thing that kept me from going crazy was that I still had you. The fact that you put your career—your whole life—on hold to come back here meant everything to me. But it tears me apart to know you're still blaming yourself. You've let your entire world shrink to this ranch because of some misplaced sense of duty."

"It's not misplaced. You're my father," Caden said, clearing his throat when his voice cracked. "You saved me."

"It was an honor to raise you." Garrett moved forward and placed a gentle hand on Caden's shoulder. "I'm proud of the man you've become despite everything you've been through. But for you to hurt Lucy—"

"Why didn't you say something to me about Derek?"

Garrett's smile was sad. "You're protective and loyal to a fault. Derek was supposed to be your brother's best friend. I wanted to be certain before I took action."

"I've screwed up so badly."

"Where's Lucy?" Maureen interrupted. "I lost my phone yesterday when we were walking through Central Park. Garrett texted Lucy to keep her updated on our arrival home, but she didn't call back or message him."

She took a shuddery breath. "She doesn't know that Garrett had flown Bobby to Colorado to force him to sign the divorce papers. She probably thinks I didn't handle anything and left her out here to deal with the fallout from my mistakes."

"Lucy is staying with a friend in Crimson. But from what I understand, she has good reason to believe that about you."

"Caden." Garrett's tone had that telltale angry-dad edge.

"He's right," Maureen admitted. "I haven't always been the best mom. I'm selfish and immature."

"Darlin', no," Garrett murmured.

"I'm trying to be a better person." She swiped under her eyes and looked straight at Caden. "Your father has a lot to do with that. But so does Lucy. She deserves better."

Caden sighed, scrubbed a hand across his jaw. "If she gives me another chance, I'm going to be the man she deserves."

Maureen turned to Garrett. "Give me your phone, hon. I have to reach her."

"Let me call," Caden said, pulling his phone from his back pocket.

Maureen lifted a brow. "Do you really think she'll want to talk to you right now?"

Caden wanted to argue, but she was right.

Maureen paced to the edge of the room as she punched in the number. "Pick up," she whispered, the phone pressed to her ear. "Pick up." She let out a little cry of relief. "Lucy-Goose, it's me. I just heard about your argument with Caden."

There was a pause, and Maureen's lips pressed into a thin line. "I know, sweetie. I'm sorry. Garrett flew him to Colorado so we could handle the divorce paperwork in person. He's agreed to sign. Garrett made sure of it. I took your advice and told him everything."

Another pause. "You were right about that, too. Caden knows we had no plan to take advantage of anyone." Her voice lowered. "He's really sorry, baby. I can tell how bad he feels about doubting you." She shook her head as she listened to something Lucy said. "You've got to drive back out to the ranch. We can work everything—" Her mouth formed a small O. "What do you mean you're gone? Where in the world is Jackrabbit Pass?"

Caden took a step forward. "That's on the other side of Crimson Mountain," he told Maureen, then glanced to the window where snow blew in frenetic circles, dancing in the light from the porch lamp. "Usually they close it in this kind of weather."

Garrett nodded. "From the time we got off the interstate and drove into town, at least two inches of snow fell. I can only imagine the conditions on Jackrab—"

He broke off as Maureen let out a startled cry.

"Lucy!" she screamed into the phone. "Are you there?"

"What happened?" Caden rushed forward and snatched the device from her hand.

"She yelled something about sliding," Maureen said, her voice shaking. "Then there was a terrible sound. Metal on metal. Like a crash."

The screen had gone dark, and he immediately punched in Lucy's number again. The call went straight to voice mail.

Caden tossed the phone to his dad and grabbed his coat. "Get a hold of Cole Bennett. See if anyone from the sheriff's department is out that way. Then try the fire department and Jeremy. They should have plows running out that way. Someone has to be close to her. Call me if Lucy contacts you."

"Where are you going?" his father asked as he reached for his phone.

"Jackrabbit Pass," Caden answered, snow billowing into the house when he opened the door. "I'm going to bring Lucy home."

It took Caden almost an hour to reach the summit, although he drove like he was qualifying for the winter version of the Indy 500.

The plows had taken care of the main highway, but as soon as he turned onto the winding, two-lane road that led up Crimson Mountain and south toward Jackrabbit Pass, conditions worsened with every passing minute.

His rear wheels lost traction several times even though his truck had studded snow tires and sandbags weighing down the back end. He couldn't imagine Lucy's cracker-box rental car driving up and over the icy pass. Hell, she must have been desperate to put miles between the two of them to attempt it.

He'd seen a couple of big SUVs making their way slowly down the curvy road, but neither of them had stopped despite him flashing his brights to flag them down.

His cell phone remained maddeningly dark where it sat on the console next to him. He didn't put a lot of stock in prayer, but he'd offered up a litany of silent pleas, mainly addressed to his brother, begging to find Lucy safe.

With his heart thudding against his ribs and tension pounding through his bloodstream, it was difficult to remember why he'd been so angry with her. He quickly realized pride and fear had mingled together to drive his reaction. It was tough to admit he'd so misjudged a man he thought was a family friend, especially after the deception by his lying, cheating ex-girlfriend had caused the rift with Tyson.

But he'd allowed his anger toward one woman to make him wrongfully mistrust another. Lucy's mother did truly love his father. He'd been so convinced that he couldn't trust any woman again, but part of that had been fear of being hurt overshadowing what his heart felt.

He loved Lucy in a way he'd never imagined himself capable of feeling. That scared the hell out of him. Love meant being hurt. But nothing could hurt as much as the thought of losing her.

He had to find her and convince her to give him another chance—to make sure she was safe.

He couldn't lose her, too.

Snow swirled in the light of the truck's lights as he started down the other side of Jackrabbit Pass. The storm raged so fast and hard that there were no other tire tracks on the road, and he was forced to slow down and pay close attention to the snow markers along the shoulder. The side of the mountain dropped off sharply on his right, with the tops of snow-covered pine trees forming a blanket across the landscape.

Although he was used to winter driving in the mountains, his whole body was rigid with tension. How the hell could Lucy handle this?

As if in answer to his question, his lights picked up the flash of taillights about a hundred yards ahead of him around the bend of a sharp switchback.

He swallowed back a rush of terror when he inched closer and recognized Lucy's car. It had crashed into the guardrail and the front quarter of the vehicle was hanging over the shoulder. He pulled off and bolted from the truck, racing through the snow and darkness toward the small car.

"Lucy," he shouted, but the only answer was the wind whistling around him.

The car looked stable, but as he got closer he noticed the driver's-side door was slightly ajar. Panic almost brought him to his knees as a hundred terrifying scenarios ran through his head.

"Lucy," he called again, shining the flashlight from his phone toward the interior of the car. A thick layer of fresh snow covered the windows, and he dusted it off, praying to find her uninjured.

"Caden?"

He whirled around at the sound of her voice behind him. Suddenly headlights from a truck he hadn't noticed when he pulled up illuminated her. Terror changed to relief but the power of what he felt still threatened to bring him to his knees.

He moved toward her, hardly believing she was real.

"How did you get here?" she asked. "The snowplow driver told me—"

He crushed his mouth against hers, needing to feel her for himself. He needed to inhale her breath into his lungs, trying to regain his footing from the emotional abyss on which he still teetered.

"You scared the hell out of me," he whispered against her skin, trailing kisses across her cheeks and over her eyelids. "You're okay?" He pulled back, cupping her face between his palms. "Tell me you're fine, Lucy."

"A little shaken up," she admitted. "And the car is in bad shape."

"Tell me—"

"I'm okay," she said, putting a finger to his lips. "I was going really slow and I know I should have pulled off, but I was—"

"Leaving me," he finished.

Her brow furrowed. "You made it clear that we had no future. You didn't trust me. You accused me of… How could you think those things? How can we ever have a chance when you're willing to believe the worst?"

Lucy was proud her voice remained steady as she asked the questions that had been plaguing her since she'd driven away from Sharpe Ranch.

She wanted to lean into Caden, to let his strength melt away the lingering terror from the drive up the mountain and the rental car's slide across the icy road and into the guardrail.

But while her time in Crimson had been short, the town and the friends she'd made there had changed her.

She'd always been satisfied with scraps of a life because she hadn't believed she deserved anything more.

Now she did, and even though she loved Caden, she wouldn't allow anyone to make her feel less than who she knew herself to be.

He studied her for several long moments, snowflakes clinging to his hair and his breath coming out in tiny clouds of air.

"I'm sorry," he said finally. "You have every reason to walk away from me, Lucy. I tend to make a mess of things with the people I love most."

She sucked in a breath, almost choking on the cold air. "You love me?"

The tips of his warm fingers melted the snowflakes that stuck to her cheeks. "I love you with everything I am, but I have a hard time believing that's enough." He closed his eyes for a moment and when he opened them again, she saw the scared little boy that had survived so much before coming to live on Sharpe Ranch. "I can't believe *I'm* enough, so it's easier to create a reason why things won't work out. Because if I end it first, the break will hurt less."

"Does it hurt less?" she asked quietly.

He shook his head. "It feels like I ripped out my own heart."

"Mine, too."

"I'm sorry I hurt you. You're everything to me, Lucy. My very own Christmas miracle, and I don't even believe in miracles. Not until you came into my life and turned it upside down. You're beautiful and smart and have the sweetest heart I could ever imagine. I know I don't deserve another chance but give me one, anyway. Please. I can do better. I will do better. I'll make you so happy."

"You already do," she told him, hope blooming warm and bright in her chest, like they were standing in a sunny field of flowers instead of on a remote mountain pass in the middle of a blizzard.

He leaned in and kissed her gently as if mending the pain he'd caused. "Will you take me on, Lucy? I promise I'll leave my idiot days in our past." The words were soft against her lips. "You're the only future I want. I can't imagine my life without you. Please say—"

"Yes," she whispered and wrapped her arms around his neck, sighing when he pulled her tight against him. "I'll give you a million chances. I love the man that you are, although we're definitely going to need to work on the idiot tendencies."

"Reformed idiot," he said with a smile. "You've reformed me."

"I wouldn't want that job to go to anyone else." She laughed as he lifted her and spun her around.

A loud whistle had them both turning to see the snowplow driver waving from the cab of his truck. "Y'all think you might want to take that lovey-dovey stuff indoors? If you haven't noticed, the snow's not letting up. We need to get off this mountain sooner than later."

"Let's go," Caden said, tucking Lucy against his side. They spoke to the driver for a few moments, and he suggested they follow him down the mountain in Caden's truck and come back for Lucy's car once the storm passed.

"I'm sorry you had to come out in this to find me," she said after they'd collected her things and climbed into the truck. Caden turned it around and pulled back onto the road.

"You never have to apologize," he answered. "There isn't anything I wouldn't do for you, Lucy. I'd drive through a thousand storms to bring you home. I love you."

"Home," she repeated, cherishing the thought of finally having a place she belonged. And knowing without a doubt that her place was with Caden. Forever.

Epilogue

"It's almost midnight," Lucy told Caden one week later as she glanced at her watch.

"Time for a New Year's Eve break," he said, plucking the paint roller from her hand.

"But we're so close." She stepped back to survey her progress. As Caden worked on installing new trim and crown molding throughout the cozy family room, Lucy had been busy painting the decades-old pine paneling a fresh shade of creamy white.

Although they'd been invited to ring in the New Year with friends in Crimson, Lucy and Caden had chosen to stay on the ranch and continue renovations on the little guesthouse behind the barn. Garrett and Maureen weren't scheduled to return from their honeymoon for another week, and Lucy wanted to make sure Caden was settled in the guesthouse before they got back. They wanted to give the newlyweds privacy and also retain some for themselves where they could.

She'd moved in with Erin MacDonald and planned to sublet her new friend's apartment once Erin and David were married over Valentine's Day weekend. As much as she loved Caden and her time with him, she felt strangely old-fashioned about living with him at the start of their relationship. Everything felt so fresh and new, and she wanted them both to have time to adjust to the changes in their lives before they moved in together.

"Can't we just count down later?" she asked. "I'm so close to finishing this wall."

"Maybe you want to rethink the business degree," Caden said with a laugh, gently taking her wrist and tugging her toward the door, "and go for your contractor's license. I've never met someone who wants to work like you, and I grew up on a ranch."

"I might consider that," she said. "Some of the online programs I'm looking at have specializations in construction management." The truth was, she loved everything about renovating the old space and turning it into something new. Although just a month ago, she would have dismissed the idea of trying a new focus for her career, she'd come to see that she had way more to offer than she'd ever realized.

"You'd be a natural," he said, pulling a coat from the rack and draping it over her shoulders. "But I believe you'd be a success at anything you set your mind to."

"I like the thought of that," she said, slipping her hand into his. They walked out into the cold, clear night and Caden led her behind the house, to the edge of the field where they had an unobstructed view of Crimson Mountain.

"It's pretty in the moonlight," she said.

"Just wait."

As if on cue, there was a loud whistling in the distance, and a bright light shot into the air from the base of the mountain. A moment later, a booming sound reverberated through the night, and fireworks exploded above the peak.

Lucy gasped with delight. "It's amazing."

Caden shifted so that he was standing behind her, and she leaned back against his chest as his arms came around her. "Happy New Year," he whispered against her ear. "I love you."

"I love you, too," she said and turned her head to kiss him, letting the happiness she'd discovered this holiday season light her heart until she flared as bright as the fireworks on Crimson Mountain. "Always and forever."

* * * * *

If you loved this book, you'll be happy to hear that Michelle Major is kicking off the newest Fortunes of Texas continuity,
**THE FORTUNES OF TEXAS:
THE RULEBREAKERS!**

*HER SOLDIER OF FORTUNE
will be released in January 2018.*

And don't miss Michelle's previous books in the
CRIMSON, COLORADO *miniseries:*

*ROMANCING THE WALLFLOWER
CHRISTMAS ON CRIMSON MOUNTAIN
ALWAYS THE BEST MAN*

*Available now wherever Harlequin Special Edition
books and ebooks are sold!*

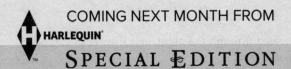

#2593 HER SOLDIER OF FORTUNE
The Fortunes of Texas: The Rulebreakers • by Michelle Major

When Nathan Fortune returned home, he vowed to put the past behind him. But when Bianca, his best friend's little sister, shows up with her son, Nate finds that the past won't stay buried...and it threatens to snuff out the future Nate and Bianca now hope to build with each other.

#2594 THE ARIZONA LAWMAN
Men of the West • by Stella Bagwell

Tessa Parker goes to Arizona to investigate her unexpected inheritance and gets more than a ranch. There's a sexy deputy next door and perhaps this orphan may finally find a family on the horizon.

#2595 JUST WHAT THE COWBOY NEEDED
The Bachelors of Blackwater Lake • by Teresa Southwick

Logan Hunt needs a nanny. What he gets is pretty kindergarten teacher Grace Flynn, whose desire for roots and a family flies right in the face of Logan's determination to remain a bachelor. Can Logan overcome his fears of becoming his father in time to convince Grace that she's exactly what he wants?

#2596 CLAIMING THE CAPTAIN'S BABY
American Heroes • by Rochelle Alers

Former army captain and current billionaire Giles Wainwright is shocked to learn he has a daughter and even more shocked at how attracted he is to her adoptive mother, Mya Lawson. But Mya doesn't trust Giles's motives when it comes to her heart and he will have to work harder than ever if he wants to claim Mya's love.

#2597 THE RANCHER AND THE CITY GIRL
Sweet Briar Sweethearts • by Kathy Douglass

Running for her life, Camille Parker heads to her sworn enemy, Jericho Jones, for protection. She may be safe from those who wish her harm, but as they both come to see their past presumptions proven incorrect, Camille's heart is more at risk than ever.

#2598 BAYSIDE'S MOST UNEXPECTED BRIDE
Saved by the Blog • by Kerri Carpenter

Riley Hudson is falling for her best friend and boss, Sawyer Wallace, the only person who knows she is the ubiquitous Bayside Blogger. Awkward as that could be, though, they both have bigger problems in the form of blackmail and threats to close down the newspaper they both work for! Will Sawyer see past that long enough to make Riley Bayside's most unexpected bride?

Get 2 Free Books,

HARLEQUIN

SPECIAL EDITION

Plus <u>2</u> Free Gifts —
just for trying the
Reader Service!

"He's an idiot," Nate offered automatically.

One side of her mouth kicked up. "You sound like
Eddie. He never liked Brett, even when we were first
dating. He said he wasn't good enough for me."

"Obviously that's true." Nate took a step closer
but stopped himself before he reached for her. Bianca
didn't belong to him, and he had no claim on her. But
one morning with EJ and he already felt a connection to
the boy. A connection he also wanted to explore with the
beautiful woman in front of him. "Any man who would
walk away from you needs to have his—" He paused,
feeling the unfamiliar sensation of color rising to his face.
His mother had certainly raised him better than to swear
in front of a lady, yet the thought of Bianca being hurt by
her ex made his blood boil. "He needs a swift kick in the
pants."

"Agreed," she said with a bright smile. A smile that

made him weak in the knees. He wanted to give her a reason to smile like that every day. "I'm better off without him, but it still makes me sad for EJ. I do my best, but it's hard with only the two of us. There are so many things we've had to sacrifice." She wrapped her arms around her waist and turned to gaze out of the barn, as if she couldn't bear to make eye contact with Nate any longer. "Sometimes I wish I could give him more."

"You're enough," he said, reaching out a hand to brush away the lone tear that tracked down her cheek. "Don't doubt for one second that you're enough."

As he'd imagined, her skin felt like velvet under his callused fingertip. Her eyes drifted shut and she tipped up her face, as if she craved his touch as much as he wanted to give it to her.

He wanted more from this woman—this moment—than he'd dreamed possible. A loose strand of hair brushed the back of his hand, sending shivers across his skin.

She glanced at him from beneath her lashes, but there was no hesitation in her gaze. Her liquid brown eyes held only invitation, and his entire world narrowed to the thought of kissing Bianca.

"I finished with the hay, Mommy," EJ called from behind him.

Don't miss
HER SOLDIER OF FORTUNE by Michelle Major,
available January 2018 wherever
Harlequin® Special Edition books and ebooks are sold.

www.Harlequin.com

HSEEXP1217

LOVE
Harlequin
romance?

Join our Harlequin community to share your thoughts and connect with other romance readers!

Be the first to find out about promotions, news, and exclusive content!

Sign up for the Harlequin e-newsletter and download a free book from any series at

www.TryHarlequin.com

CONNECT WITH US AT:

Harlequin.com/Community

 Facebook.com/HarlequinBooks

 Twitter.com/HarlequinBooks

 Instagram.com/HarlequinBooks

 Pinterest.com/HarlequinBooks

ReaderService.com

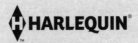

**ROMANCE WHEN
YOU NEED IT**

HSOCIAL2017

THE WORLD IS BETTER WITH

Romance

Harlequin has everything from contemporary, passionate and heartwarming to suspenseful and inspirational stories.

Whatever your mood, we have a romance just for you!

Connect with us to find your next great read, special offers and more.

 /HarlequinBooks

 @HarlequinBooks

www.HarlequinBlog.com

www.Harlequin.com/Newsletters

HARLEQUIN

A *Romance* FOR EVERY MOOD™

www.Harlequin.com

Looking for more satisfying love stories
with community and family at their core?

Check out **Harlequin® Special Edition**
and **Harlequin® Western Romance** books!

New books available every month!

CONNECT WITH US AT:

Harlequin.com/Community

Facebook.com/HarlequinBooks

Twitter.com/HarlequinBooks

Instagram.com/HarlequinBooks

Pinterest.com/HarlequinBooks

ReaderService.com

ROMANCE WHEN
YOU NEED IT

HFGENRE2017R